IN EXILE
and Other Stories

CLASSICS FROM WILDSIDE PRESS

Blix, by Frank Norris
Moran of the 'Lady Letty', by Frank Norris

IN EXILE
and Other Stories

MARY HALLOCK FOOTE

WILDSIDE PRESS

IN EXILE AND OTHER STORIES

Published by:
Wildside Press
P.O. Box 301
Holicong, PA 18928-0301 USA
www.wildsidepress.com

CONTENTS

IN EXILE

I

Nicky Dyer and the schoolmistress sat upon the slope of a hill, one of a low range overlooking an arid Californian valley. These sunburnt slopes were traversed by many narrow footpaths, descending, ascending, winding among the tangle of poison-oak and wild-rose bushes, leading from the miners' cabins to the shaft-houses and tunnels of the mine which gave to the hills their only importance. Nicky was a stout Cornish lad of thirteen, with large light eyes that seemed mildly to protest against the sportive relation which a broad, freckled, turned-up nose bore to the rest of his countenance; he was doing nothing in particular, and did it as if he were used to it. The schoolmistress sat with her skirts tucked round her ankles, the heels of her stout little boots driven well into the dry, gritty soil. There was in her attitude the tension of some slight habitual strain—perhaps of endurance—as she leaned forward, her arms stretched straight before her, with her delicate fingers interlocked. Whatever may be the type of Californian young womanhood, it was not her type; you felt, looking at her cool, clear tints and slight, straight outlines, that she had winter in her blood.

She was gazing down into the valley, as one looks at a landscape who has not yet mastered all its changes of expression; its details were blurred in the hot, dusty glare; the mountains opposite had faded to a flat outline against the indomitable sky. A light wind blew up the slope, flickering the pale leaves of a manzanita, whose burnished, cinnamon-colored stems glowed in the sun. As the breeze strengthened, the young girl stood up, lifting her arms, to welcome its coolness on her bare wrists.

"Nicky, why do the trees in that hollow between the hills look so green?"

"There'll be water over there, miss; that's the Chilano's spring. I'm thinkin' the old cow might 'a' strayed over that way somewheres; they mostly goes for the water, wherever it is."

"Is it running water, Nicky—not water in a tank?"

"Why, no, miss; it cooms right out o' the rock as pretty as iver you saw! I often goes there myself for a drink, cos it tastes sort o' different, coomin' out o' the ground like. We wos used to that kind o' water at 'ome."

"Let us go, Nicky," said the girl. "I should like to taste that water, too. Do we cross the hill first, or is there a shorter way?"

"Over the 'ill's the shortest, miss. It's a bit of a ways, but you've been longer ways nor they for less at th' end on't."

They "tacked" down the steepest part of the hill, and waded through a shady hollow, where ferns grew rank and tall—crisp, faded ferns, with an aromatic odor which escaped by the friction of their garments, like the perfume of warmed amber. They reached at length the green trees, a clump of young cottonwoods at the entrance to a narrow canon, and followed the dry bed of a stream for some distance, until water began to show among the stones. The principal outlet of the spring was on a small plantation at the head of the canon, rented of the "company" by a Chilian, or "the Chilano," as he was called; he was not at all a pastoral-looking personage, but, with the aid of his good water, he earned a moderately respectable living by supplying the neighboring cabins and the miners' boarding-house with green vegetables. After a temporary disappearance, as if to purge its memory of the Chilano's water-buckets, the spring again revealed itself in a thin, clear trickle down the hollowed surface of a rock which closed the narrow passage of the canon. Young sycamores and cottonwoods shut out the sun above; their tangled roots, interlaced with vines still green and growing, trailed over the edge of the rock, where a mass of earth had fallen; green moss lined the hollows of the rock, and water-plants grew in the dark pools below.

The strollers had left behind them the heat and glare; only the breeze followed them into this green stillness, stirring the boughs overhead and scattering spots of sunlight over the wet stones. Nicky, after enjoying for a few moments the schoolmistress' surprised delight, proposed that she should wait for him at the spring, while he went "down along" in search of his cow. Nicky was not without a certain awe of the schoolmistress, as a part of creation he had not fathomed in all its bearings; but when they rambled on the hills together, he found himself less uneasily conscious of her personality, and more comfortably aware of the fact that, after all, she was "nothin' but a woman." He was a trifle disappointed that she showed no uneasiness at being left alone, but consoled himself by the reflection that she was "a good un to 'old 'er tongue," and probably felt more than she expressed.

The schoolmistress did not look in the least disconsolate after Nicky's departure. She gazed about her very contentedly for a while, and then prepared to help herself to a drink of water. She hollowed her two hands into a cup, and waited for it to fill, stooping below the rock, her lifted skirt held against her side by one elbow, while she watched with a childish eagerness the water trickle into her pink palms. Miss Frances Newell had never looked prettier in her life. A pretty girl is always prettier in the open air, with her head uncovered. Her cheeks were red; the sun just touched the roughened braids of dark brown hair, and intensified the glow of a little ear which showed beneath. She stooped to drink; but Miss Frances was destined never to taste that virgin cup of water. There was a trampling among the bushes, overhead; a little shower of dust and pebbles pattered down upon her bent head, soiling the water. She let her hands fall as she looked up, with a startled "Oh!" A pair of large boots were rapidly making their way down the bank, and the cause of all this disturbance stood before her,— a young man in a canvas jacket, with a leathern case slung across his shoulder, and a small tin lamp fastened in front of the hat which he took off while he apologized to the girl for his intrusion.

"Miss Newell! Forgive me for dropping down on you like a thousand of brick! You've found the spring, I see."

Miss Frances stood with her elbows still pressed to her sides, though her skirt had slipped down into the water, her wet palms helplessly extended. "I was getting a drink," she said, searching with the tips of her fingers among the folds of her dress for a handkerchief. "You came just in time to remind me of the slip between the cup and the lip."

"I'm very sorry, but there is plenty of water left. I came for some myself. Let me help you." He took from one of the many pockets stitched into the breast and sides of his jacket a covered flask, detached the cup, and, after carefully rinsing, filled and handed it to the girl. "I hope it doesn't taste of 'store claret;' the water underground is just a shade worse than that exalted vintage."

"It is delicious, thank you, and it doesn't taste in the least of claret. Have you just come out of the mine?"

"Yes. It is measuring-up day. I've been toddling through the drifts and sliding down chiflons—" he looked ruefully at the backs of his trousers legs—"ever since seven o'clock this morning. Haven't had time to eat any luncheon yet, you see." He took from another pocket a small package folded in a coarse napkin. "I came here to satisfy the pangs of hunger and enjoy the beauties of nature at the same time—such nature as we have here. Will you excuse me, Miss Newell? I'll promise to eat very fast."

"I'll excuse you if you will not ask me to eat with you."

"Oh, I've entirely too much consideration for myself to think of such a thing; there isn't enough for two."

He seated himself, with a little sigh, and opened the napkin on the ground before him. Miss Newell stood leaning against a rock on the opposite side of the brook, regarding the young man with a shy and smiling curiosity. "Meals," he continued, "are a reckless tribute to the weakness of the flesh we all engage in three times a day at the boarding-house; a man must eat, you know, if he expects to live. Have you ever tried any of Mrs. Bondy's fare, Miss Newell?"

"I'm sure Mrs. Bondy tries to have everything very nice," the young girl replied, with some embarrassment.

"Of course she does; she is a very good old girl. I think a great deal of Mrs. Bondy; but when she asks me if I have enjoyed my dinner, I always make a point of telling her the truth; she respects me for it. This is her idea of sponge cake, you see." He held up admiringly a damp slab of some compact pale-yellow substance, with crumbs of bread adhering to one side. "It is a little mashed, but otherwise a fair specimen."

Miss Frances laughed. "Mr. Arnold, I think you are too bad. How can she help it, with those dreadful Chinamen? But I would really advise you not to eat that cake; it doesn't look wholesome."

"Oh, as to that, I've never observed any difference; one thing is about as wholesome as another. Did you ever eat bacon fried by China Sam? The sandwiches were made of that. You see I still live." The sponge cake was rapidly disappearing. "Miss Newell, you look at me as if I were making away with myself, instead of the cake—will you appear at the inquest?"

"No, I will not testify to anything so unromantic; besides, it might be inconvenient for Mrs. Bondy's cook." She put on her hat, and stepped along the stones towards the entrance to the glen.

"You are not going to refuse me the last offices?"

"I am going to look for Nicky Dyer. He came with me to show me the spring, and now he has gone to hunt for his cow."

"And you are going to hunt for him? I hope you won't try it, Miss Frances: a boy on the track of a cow is a very uncertain object in life. Let me call him, if you really must have him."

"Oh, don't trouble yourself. I suppose he will come after a while. I said I would wait for him here."

"Then permit me to say that I think you had better do as you promised."

Miss Frances recrossed the stones, and seated herself, with a faint deprecatory smile.

"I hope you don't mind if I stay," Arnold said, moving some loose stones to make her seat more comfortable. "You have the prior right today, but this is an old haunt of mine. I feel as if I were doing the honors; and to tell you the truth, I am rather used up. The new workings are very hot and the drifts are low. It's a combination of steam-bath and hoeing corn."

The girl's face cleared, as she looked at him. His thin cheek was pale under the tan, and where his hat was pushed back the hair clung in damp points to his forehead and temples.

"I should be very sorry to drive you away," she said. "I thought you looked tired. If you want to go to sleep, or anything, I will promise to be very quiet."

Arnold laughed. "Oh, I'm not such an utter wreck; but I'm glad you can be very quiet. I was afraid you might be a little uproarious at times, you know."

The girl gave a sudden shy laugh. It was really a giggle, but a very sweet, girlish giggle. It called up a look of keen pleasure to Arnold's face.

"Now I call this decidedly gay," he remarked, stretching out his long legs slowly, and leaning against a slanting rock, with one arm behind his head. "Miss Frances, will you be good enough to tell me that my face isn't dirty?"

"Truth compels me to admit that you have one little daub over your left eyebrow."

"Thank you," said Arnold, rubbing it languidly with his handkerchief. His hat had dropped off, and he did not replace it; he did not look at the girl, but let his eyes rest on the thread of falling water that gleamed from the spring. Miss Frances, regarding him with some timidity, thought: How much younger he looks without his hat! He had that sensitive fairness which in itself gives a look of youth and purity; the sternness of his face lay in the curves which showed under his mustache, and in the silent, dominant eye.

"You've no idea how good it sounds to a lonely fellow like me," he said, "to hear a girl's laugh."

"But there are a great many women here," Miss Frances observed.

"Oh yes, there are women everywhere, such as they are; but it takes a nice girl, a lady, to laugh!"

"I don't agree with you at all," replied Miss Frances coldly. "Some of those Mexican women have the sweetest voices, speaking or laughing, that I have ever heard; and the Cornish women, too, have very fresh, pure voices. I often listen to them in the evening when I sit alone in my room. Their voices sound so happy—"

"Well, then it is the home accent—or I'm prejudiced. Don't laugh again, please, Miss Frances; it breaks me all up." He moved his head a little, and looked across at the girl to assure himself that her silence did not mean disapproval. "I admit," he went on, "that I like our Eastern girls. I know you are from the East, Miss Newell."

"I am from what I used to think was East," she said, smiling. "But everything is East here; people from Indiana and Wisconsin say they are from the East."

"Ah, but you are from our old Atlantic coast. I was sure of it when I first saw you. If you will pardon me, I knew it by your way of dressing."

The young girl flushed with pleasure; then, with a reflective air: "I confess myself, since you speak of clothes, to a feeling of relief when I saw your hat the first Sunday after I came. Western men wear such dreadful hats."

"Good!" he cried gayly. "You mean my hat that I *call* a hat." He reached for the one behind his head, and spun it lightly upward, where it settled on a projecting branch. "I respect that hat myself—my *other* hat, I mean; I'm trying to live up to it. Now, let me guess your State, Miss Newell: is it Massachusetts?"

"No—Connecticut; but at this distance it seems like the same thing."

"Oh, pardon me, there are very decided differences. I'm from Massachusetts myself. Perhaps the points of difference show more in the women—the ones who stay at home, I mean, and become more local and idiomatic than the men. You are not one of the daughters of the soil, Miss Newell."

She looked pained as she said, "I wish I were; but there is not room for us all, where there is so little soil."

Arnold moved uneasily, extracted a stone from under the small of his back and tossed it out of sight with some vehemence. "You think it goes rather hard with women who are uprooted, then," he said. "I suppose it is something a roving man can hardly conceive of—a woman's attachment to places, and objects, and associations; they are like cats."

Miss Newell was silent.

Arnold moved restlessly; then began again, with his eyes still on the trickle of water: "Miss Newell, do you remember a poem—I think it is Bryant's—called 'The Hunter of the Prairies'? It's no disgrace not to remember it, and it may not be Bryant's."

"I remember seeing it, but I never read it. I always skipped those Western things."

Arnold gave a short laugh, and said, "Well, you are punished, you see, by going West yourself to hear me repeat it to you. I think I can give you the idea in the Hunter's own words:—

> "*'Here, with my rifle and my steed,*
> *And her who left the world for me'—*"

The sound of his own voice in the stillness of the little glen, and a look of surprise in the young girl's quiet eyes, brought a sudden access of color to Arnold's face. "Hm-m-m," he murmured to himself, "it's queer how rhymes slip away. Well, the last line ends in *free*. You see, it is a man's idea of happiness—a young man's. Now, how do you suppose *she* liked it— the girl, you know, who left the world, and all that? Did you ever happen to see a poem or a story, written by a woman, celebrating the joys of a solitary existence with the man of her heart?"

"I suppose that many a woman has tried it," Miss Newell said evasively, "but I'm sure she—"

"Never lived to tell the tale?" cried Arnold.

"She probably had something else to do, while the hunter was riding around with his gun," Miss Frances continued.

"Well, give her the odds of the rifle and the steed; give the man some commonplace employment to take the swagger out of him; let him come home reasonably tired and cross at night—do you suppose he would find the 'kind' eyes and the 'smile'? I forgot to tell you that the Hunter of the Prairies is always welcomed by a smile at night."

"He must have been an uncommonly fortunate man," she said.

"Of course he was; but the question is: Could any living man be so fortunate? Come, Miss Frances, don't prevaricate!"

"Well, am I speaking for the average woman?"

"Oh, not at all—you are speaking for the very nicest of women; any other kind would be intolerable on a prairie."

"I should think, if she were very healthy," said Miss Newell, hesitating between mischief and shyness, "and not too imaginative, and of a cheerful disposition; and if he, the hunter, were above the average—supposing that she cared for him in the beginning—I should think the smile might last a year or two."

"Heavens, what a cynic you are! I feel like a mere daub of sentiment beside you. There have been moments, do you know, even in this benighted mining camp, when I have believed in that hunter and his smile!"

He got up suddenly, and stood against the rock, facing her. Although he kept his cool, bantering tone, his breathing had quickened, and his eyes looked darker.

"You may consider me a representative man, if you please: I speak for hundreds of us scattered about in mining camps and on cattle ranches, in lighthouses and frontier farms and military posts, and all the Godforsaken holes you can conceive of, where men are trying to earn a living, or lose one—we are all going to the dogs for the want of that smile! What is to become of us if the women whose smiles we care for cannot support life in the places where we have to live? Come, Miss Frances, can't you make that smile last at least two years?" He gathered a handful of dry leaves from a broken branch above his head and crushed them in his long hands, sifting the yellow dust upon the water below.

"The places you speak of are very different," the girl answered, with a shade of uneasiness in her manner. "A mining camp is anything but a solitude, and a military post may be very gay."

"Oh, the principle is the same. It is the absolute giving up of everything. You know most women require a background of family and friends and congenial surroundings; the question is whether *any* woman can do without them."

The young girl moved in a constrained way, and flushed as she said, "It must always be an experiment, I suppose, and its success would depend, as I said before, on the woman and on the man."

"An 'experiment' is good!" said Arnold, rather savagely. "I see you won't say anything you can't swear to."

"I really do not see that I am called upon to say anything on the subject at all!" said the girl, rising and looking at him across the brook with indignant eyes and a hot glow on her cheek.

He did not appear to notice her annoyance.

"You are, because you know something about it, and most women don't: your testimony is worth something. How long have you been here—a year? I wonder how it seems to a woman to live in a place like this a year! I hate it all, you know—I've seen so much of it. But is there really any beauty here? I suppose beauty, and all that sort of thing, is partly within us, isn't it?—at least, that's what the goody little poems tell us."

"I think it is very beautiful here," said Miss Frances, softening, as he laid aside his strained manner, and spoke more quietly. "It is the kind of place a happy woman might be very happy in; but if she were sad—or—disappointed—"

"Well?" said Arnold, pulling at his mustache, and fixing a rather gloomy gaze upon her.

"She would die of it! I really do not think there would be any hope for her in a place like this."

"But if she were happy, as you say," persisted the young man, "don't you think her woman's adaptability and quick imagination would help her immensely? She wouldn't see what I, for instance, know to be ugly and coarse; her very ignorance of the world would help her."

There was a vague, pleading look in his eyes. "Arrange it to suit yourself," she said. "Only, I can assure you, if anything should happen to her, it will be the—the hunter's fault."

"All right," said he, rousing himself. "That hunter, if I know him, is a man who is used to taking risks! Where are you going?"

"I thought I heard Nicky."

They were both silent, and as they listened, footsteps, with a tinkling accompaniment, crackled among the bushes below the canon. Miss Newell turned towards the spring again.

"I want one more drink before I go," she said.

Arnold followed her. "Let us drink to our return. Let this be our fountain of Trevi."

"Oh, no," said Miss Frances. "Don't you remember what your favorite Bryant says about bringing the 'faded fancies of an elder world' into these 'virgin solitudes'?"

"Faded fancies!" cried Arnold. "Do you call that a faded fancy? It is as fresh and graceful as youth itself, and as natural. I should have thought of it myself, if there had been no fountain of Trevi."

"Do you think so?" smiled the girl. "Then imagination, it would seem, is not entirely confined to homesick women."

"Come, fill the cup, Miss Frances! Nicky is almost here."

The girl held her hands beneath the trickle again, until they were brimming with the clear sweet water.

"Drink first," said Arnold.

"I'm not sure that I want to return," she replied, smiling, with her eyes on the space of sky between the treetops.

"Nonsense—you must be morbid. Drink, drink!"

"Drink yourself; the water is all running away!"

He bent his head, and took a vigorous sip of the water, holding his hands beneath hers, inclosing the small cup in the larger one. The small cup trembled a little. He was laughing and wiping his mustache, when Nicky appeared; and Miss Frances, suddenly brightening and recovering her freedom of movement, exclaimed, "Why, Nicky! You have been *forever*! We must go at once, Mr. Arnold; so good-by! I hope—"

She did not say what she hoped, and Arnold, after looking at her with an interrogative smile a moment, caught his hat from the branch overhead, and made her a great flourishing bow with it in his hand.

He did not follow her, pushing her way through the swaying, rustling ferns, but he watched her light figure out of sight. "What an extraordinary ass I've been making of myself!" He confided this remark to the stillness of the little canon, and then, with long strides, took his way over the hills in an opposite direction.

It was the middle of July when this little episode of the spring occurred. The summer had reached its climax. The dust did not grow perceptibly deeper, nor the fields browner, during the long brazen weeks that followed; one only wearied of it all, more and more.

So thought Miss Newell, at least. It was her second summer in California, and the phenomenon of the dry season was not so impressive on its repetition. She had been surprised to observe how very brief had been the charm of strangeness, in her experience of life in a new country. She began to wonder if a girl, born and brought up among the hills of Connecticut, could have the seeds of *ennui* subtly distributed through her frame, to reach a sudden development in the heat of a Californian summer. She longed for the rains to begin, that in their violence and the sound of the wind she might gain a sense of life in action by which to eke out her dull and expressionless days. She was, as Nicky Dyer had said, "a good un to 'old 'er tongue," and therein lay her greatest strength as well as her greatest danger.

Miss Newell boarded at Captain Dyer's. The prosperous ex-mining captain was a good deal nearer to the primitive type than any man Miss Newell had ever sat at table with in her life before, but she had a thorough respect for him, and she felt that the time might come when she could enjoy him—as a reminiscence. Mrs. Dyer was kindly, and not more of a gossip than her neighbors; and there were no children—only one grandchild, the inoffensive Nicky. The ways of the house were somewhat uncouth, but everything was clean and in a certain sense homelike. To Miss Newell's homesick sensitiveness it seemed better than being stared at across the boarding-house table by Boker and Pratt, and pitied by the engineer. She had a little room at the Dyers', which was a reflection of herself so far as a year's occupancy and very moderate resources could make it; perhaps for that very reason she often found her little room an intolerable prison. One night her homesickness had taken its worst form, a restlessness, which began in a nervous inward throbbing and extended to her cold and tremulous finger-tips. She went softly downstairs and out on the piazza, where the moonlight lay in a brilliant square on the unpainted boards. The moonlight increased her restlessness, but she could not keep away from it. She dared not walk up and down the piazza, because the people in the street below would see her; she stood there perfectly still, holding her elbows with her hands, crouched into a little dark heap against the side of the house.

Lights were twinkling, far and near, over the hills, singly, and in clusters. Black figures moved across the moonlit spaces in the street. There were sounds of talking, laughing, and singing; dogs barking; occasionally a stir and tinkle in the scrub, as a cow wandered past. The engines throbbed from the distant shaft-houses. A miner's wife was hushing her baby in the next house, and across the street a group of Mexicans were talking all at once in a loud, monotonous cadence.

In her early days at the mines there had been a certain piquancy in her sense of the contrast between herself and her circumstances, but that had long passed into a dreary recognition of the fact that she had no real part in the life of the place.

She recalled one afternoon when Arnold had passed the schoolhouse, and found her sitting alone on the doorstep. He had stopped to ask if that "mongrel pack on the hill were worrying the life out of her," and had added with a laugh, in answer to her look of silent disapproval, "Oh, I mean the dear lambs of your flock. I saw two of them just now on the trail, fighting over a lame donkey. The clans were gathering on both sides; there will be a pitched battle in a few minutes. The donkey was enjoying it. I think he was asleep!" The day had been an unusually hard one, and the patient little schoolmistress was just then struggling with a distracted sense of unavailing effort. Arnold's grim banter had brought the tears, as blood follows a blow. He got down from his horse, looking wretched at what he had done. "I am a brute, I believe—worse than any of the pack. You have so much patience with them—please have a little with me. Trust me, I am not utterly blind to your sufferings. Indeed, Miss Newell, I see them, and they make me savage!" With the gentlest touch he had lifted her hand, held it in his a moment, and then had mounted his horse and ridden away.

Yes, he *did* understand—she felt sure of that. What an unutterable rest it would be if she could go to some one with the small worries of her life! But she could not yield to such impulses. It was different with men. She had often thought of Arnold's words that day at the spring, all the more that he had never, before or since, revealed so much of himself to her. Under an apparently careless frankness and extravagance of speech he was a reticent man; but lightly spoken as the words had been, were they not the sparks and ashes blown from a deep and smothered core of fire? She seemed to feel its glow on her cheek as she recalled his singular persistence and the darkening of his imperious eyes. No, she would not permit herself to think of that day at the spring.

There was a bright light in the engineer's office across the street. She could see Arnold through the windows (for, like a man, he did not pull his shades down) at one of the long drawing-tables. He worked late, it seemed. He was writing; he wrote rapidly page after page, tearing each sheet from what appeared to be a paper block, and tossing it on the table beside him; he covered only one side of the paper, she noticed, thinking with a smile of her own small economies. Presently he got up, swept the papers together in his hands, and stooped over them. He is numbering and folding them, she thought, and now he is directing the envelope—to whom, I wonder! He turned, and as he walked towards the window she saw him put something into the pocket of his coat. He lighted a cigar, and began walking, with long strides, up and down the room, one hand in his pocket; the other he occasionally rubbed over his eyes and head, as if they hurt him. She remembered that the engineer had headaches, and wished that somebody would ask him to try valerian. Is he ever really lonely? she thought. What can he, what can any man, know of loneliness? He may go out and walk about on the hills; he may go away altogether, and take the risks of life somewhere else. A woman must take no risks. There is not a house in the camp where he might not enter tonight, if he chose; he might come over here and talk to me. The East, with all its cherished memories and prejudices and associations, seemed so hopelessly far away; they two alone, in that strange, uncongenial new world which had crowded out the old, seemed to speak a common language: and yet how little she really knew of him!

Suddenly the lights disappeared from the windows of the office. She heard a door unlock, and presently the young man's figure crossed the street and turned up the trail past the house.

Two other figures going up halted, and the taller one said, "Will you go up on the hill, tonight, Arnold?"

"What for?" said Arnold, slackening his pace without stopping.

"Oh, nothing in particular—to see the senoritas."

"Oh, thank you, Boker, I've seen the senoritas."

He walked quickly past the men, and the shorter one, who had not spoken, called after him rather huskily—

"W-what do you think of the little school-ma'am?"

Arnold turned back and confronted the speaker in silence.

"I say! Is she thin 'nough to suit you?" the heavy-playful one persisted.

"Shut up, Jack!" said his comrade. "You're a little high now, you know."

He dragged him on, up the trail; the voices of the two men blended with the night chorus of the camp as they passed out of sight.

Miss Newell sat perfectly still for a while; then she went to her room, and threw herself down on the bed, listening to an endless mental repetition of those words that the faithless night had brought to her ear. The moonlight had left the piazza, and crept round to the side of the house; it shone in at the window, touching the girl's cold fingers pressed to her burning cheeks and temples. She got up, drew the curtain, and groped her way back to the bed, where she lay for hours, trying to convince herself that her misery was out of all proportion to the cause, and that those coarse words could make no real difference in her life.

They did make a little difference: they loosened the slight, indefinite threads of intercourse which a year had woven between these two exiles. Miss Newell was prepared to withdraw from any further overtures of friendship from the engineer; but he made it unnecessary for her to do so— he made no overtures. On the night of Pratt's tipsy salutation he had abruptly decided that a mining camp was no place for a nice girl, with no acknowledged masculine protector. In Miss Newell's circumstances a girl must be left entirely alone, or exposed to the gossip of the camp. He knew very well which she would choose, and so he kept away—though at considerable loss to himself, he felt. It made him cross to watch her pretty figure going up the trail every morning and to reflect that so much sweetness and refinement should not be having its ameliorating influence on his own barren and somewhat defiant existence.

II

The autumn rains set in early, and the winter was unusually severe. Arnold had a purpose which kept him hard at work and very happy in those days.

During the long December nights he was shut up in his office, plodding over his maps and papers, or smoking in dreamy comfort by the fire.

He was seldom interrupted, for he had earned the character of a social ingrate and hardened recluse in the camp. He had earned it quite unconsciously, and was as little troubled by the fact as by its consequences. On the evening of New Year's Day he crossed the street to the Dyers' and asked for Miss Newell. She presently greeted him in the parlor, where she looked, Arnold thought, more than ever out of place, among the bead baskets, and splint frames inclosing photographs of deceased members of the Dyer family, and the pallid walls, weak-legged chairs, and crude imaginings in worsted work. Her apparent unconsciousness of these abominations was another source of irritation. It is always irritating to a man to see a charming woman in an unhappy and false position, where he is powerless to help her. Arnold had not expected that it would be a very exhilarating occasion—he remembered the Dyer parlor—but it was even less pleasant than he had expected. He sat down, carefully, in a glued chair whose joints had opened with the dry season and refused to close again; he did not know where the transfer of his person might end. Captain Dyer was present, and told a great many stories in a loud, tiring voice. Miss Frances sat by with some soft white knitting in her hands, and her attitude of patient attention made Arnold long to attack her with some savage pleasantries on the subject of Christmas in a mining camp; it seemed to him that patience was a virtue that could be carried too far, even in woman. Then Mrs. Dyer came in, and manoeuvred her husband out into the passage; after some loudly suggestive whispering there, she succeeded in getting him into the kitchen, and shut the door. Arnold got up soon after that, and said good-evening.

Miss Newell remained in the parlor for some time, after he had gone, moving softly about. She had gathered her knitting closely into her clasped hands; the ball trailed after her, among the legs of the chairs, and when in her silent promenade she had spun a grievous tangle of wool she sat down, and dropped the work out of her hands with a helpless gesture. Her head drooped, and tears trickled slowly between the slender white fingers which covered her face. Presently the fingers descended to her throat and clasped it close, as if to still an intolerable throbbing ache which her half-suppressed tears had left.

At length she rose, picked up her work, and patiently followed the tangled clue until she had recovered her ball; then she wound it all up neatly, wrapped the knitting in a thin white handkerchief, and went to her room.

With the fine March weather—fine in spite of the light rains—the engineer was laying out a road to the new shaft; it wound along the hillside where Miss Newell had first seen the green trees, by the spring. The engineer's orders included the building of a flume, carrying the water down from the Chilano's plantation into a tank, built on the ruins of the rock which had guarded the sylvan spring. The discordant voices of a gang of Chinamen profaned the stillness which had framed Miss Frances' girlish laughter; the blasting of the rock had loosened, to their fall, the clustering trees above, and the brook below was a mass of trampled mud.

The engineer's visits to the spring gave him no pleasure, in those days. He felt that he was the inevitable instrument of its desecration; but over the hill, just in sight from the spring, carpenters were putting a new piazza round a cottage that stood remote from the camp, where a spur of the hills descended steeply towards the valley. Arnold took a great interest in this cottage. He was frequently to be seen there in the evening, tramping up and down the new piazza, and offering to the moon, that looked in through the boughs of a live-oak at the end of the gallery, the incense of his lonely cigar. Sometimes he would take the key of the front door from his pocket, enter the silent house, and wander from one room to another, like a restless but not unhappy ghost; the moonlight, touching his face, showed it strangely stirred and softened. His was no melancholy madness.

Arnold was leaning on the gate of this cottage, one afternoon, when the schoolmistress came down the trail from the camp. She did not appear to see him, but turned off from the trail at a little distance from the cottage, and took her way across the hill behind it. Arnold watched her a few minutes, and then followed, overtaking her on the hills above the new road, where she had sat with Nicky Dyer nearly a year ago.

"I don't like to see you wandering about here, alone," he said. "The men on the road are a scratch gang, picked up anyhow, not like the regular miners. I hope you are not going to the spring!"

"Why?" said she. "Did you not drink to our return?"

"But you would not drink with me, so the spell did not work; and now the spring is gone—all its beauty, I mean. The water is there, in a tank, where the Chinamen fill their buckets night and morning, and the teamsters water their horses. We'll go over there, if you would like to see the march of modern improvements."

"No," she said; "I had rather remember it as it was; still, I don't believe in being sentimental about such things. Let us sit down a while."

A vague depression, which Arnold had been aware of in her manner when they met, became suddenly manifest in her paleness and in a look of dull pain in her eyes.

"But you are hurt about it," he said. "I wish I hadn't told you in that brutal way. I'm afraid I'm not many degrees removed from the primeval savage, after all."

"Oh, you needn't mind," she said, after a moment. "That was the only place I cared for, here, so now there will be nothing to regret when I go away."

"Are you going away, then? I'm very sorry to hear it; but of course I'm not surprised. You couldn't be expected to stand it another year; those children must have been something fearful."

"Oh, it wasn't the children."

"Well, I'm sorry. I had hoped—"

"Yes," said she, with a modest interrogation, as he hesitated, "what is it you had hoped?"

"That I might indirectly be the means of making your life less lonely here. You remember that 'experiment' we talked about at the spring?"

"That *you* talked about, you mean."

"I am going to try it myself. Not because you were so encouraging—but—it's a risk anyway, you know, and I'm not sure the circumstances make so much difference. I've known people to be wretched with all the modern conveniences. I am going East for her in about two weeks. How sorry she will be to find you gone! I wrote to her about you. You might have helped each other; couldn't you stand it, Miss Newell, don't you think, if you had another girl?"

"I'm afraid not," she said very gently. "I *must* go home. You may be sure she will not need me; you must see to it that she doesn't need—any one."

They were walking back and forth on the hill.

"I was just looking for the cottonwood-trees; are they gone too?" she asked.

"Oh yes; there isn't a tree left in the canon. Don't you envy me my work?"

"I suppose everything we do seems like desecration to somebody. Here am I making history very rapidly for this colony of ants." She looked down with a rueful smile as she spoke.

"I wish you had the history of the entire species under your foot, and could finish it at once."

"I'm not sure that I would; I'm not so fond of extermination as you pretend to be."

"Well, keep the ants if you like them, but I am firm on the subject of the camp children. There *are* blessings that brighten as they take their flight. I pay my monthly assessment for the doctor with the greatest cheerfulness; if it wasn't for him, in this climate, they would crowd us off the hill."

"Please don't!" she said wearily. "Even *I* don't like to hear you talk like that; I am sure *she* will not."

He laughed softly. "You have often reminded me of her in little ways: that was what upset me at the spring. I was very near telling you all about her that day."

"I wish that you had!" she said. They were walking towards home now. "I suppose you know it is talked of in the camp," she said, after a pause. "Mr. Dyer told me, and showed me the house, a week ago. And now I must tell you about my violets. I had them in a box in my room all winter. I should like to leave them as a little welcome to her. Last night Nicky Dyer and I planted them on the bank by the piazza under the climbing-rose; it was a secret between Nicky and me, and Nicky promised to water them until she came; but of course I meant to tell you. Will you look at them tonight, please, and see if Nicky has been faithful?"

"I will, indeed," said Arnold. "That is just the kind of thing she will delight in. If you are going East, Miss Newell, shall we not be fellow-travelers? I should be so glad to be of any service."

"No, thank you. I am to spend a month in Santa Barbara, and escort an invalid friend home. I shall have to say good-by, now. Don't go any farther with me, please."

That night Arnold mused late, leaning over the railing of the new piazza in the moonlight. He fancied that a faint perfume of violets came from the damp earth below; but it could have been only fancy, for when he searched the bank for them they were not there. The new sod was trampled, and a few leaves and slight, uptorn roots lay scattered about, with some broken twigs from the climbing-rose. He had found the gate open when he came, and the Dyer cow had passed him, meandering peacefully up the trail.

*   *   *   *   *

The crescent moon had waxed and waned since the night when it lighted the engineer's musings through the wind-parted live-oak boughs, and another slender bow gleamed in the pale, tinted haze of twilight. The month had gone, like a feverish dream, to the young schoolmistress, as she lay in her small, upper chamber, unconscious of all save alternate light and darkness, and rest following pain. When, at last, she crept down the short staircase to breathe the evening coolness, clinging to the stair-rail and holding her soft white draperies close around her, she saw the pink light lingering on the mountains, and heard the chorus to the "Sweet By and By" from the miners' chapel on the hill. It was Sunday evening, and the house was piously "emptied of its folk." She took her old seat by the parlor window, and looked across to the engineer's office; its windows and doors were shut, and the dogs of the camp were chasing each other over the loose boards of the piazza floor. She laughed a weak, convulsive laugh, thinking of the engineer's sallies of old upon that band of Ishmaelites, and of the scrambling, yelping rush that followed. He must have gone East, else the dogs had not been so bold. She looked down the valley where the mountains parted seaward, the only break in the continuous barrier of land that cut off her retreat and closed in about the atom of her own identity. The thought of that immensity of distance made her faint.

There were steps on the porch—not Captain Dyer's, for he and his good wife were lending their voices to swell the stentorian chorus that was shaking the church on the hill; the footsteps paused at the door, and Arnold himself opened it. He had not, evidently, expected to see her.

"I was looking for some one to ask about you," he said. "Are you sure you are able to be down?"

"Oh yes. I've been sitting up for several days. I wanted to see the mountains again."

He was looking at her intently, while she flushed with weakness, and drew the fringes of her shawl over her tremulous hands.

"How ill you have been! I have wished myself a woman, that I might do something for you! I suppose Mrs. Dyer nursed you like a horse."

"Oh no; she was very good; but I don't remember much about the worst of it. I thought you had gone home."

"Home! Where do you mean? I didn't know that I had ever boasted of any reserved rights of that kind. I have no mortgage, in fact or sentiment, on any part of the earth's surface, that I'm acquainted with!"

He spoke with a hard carelessness in his manner which make her shrink.

"I mean the East. I am homeless, too, but all the East seems like home to me."

"You had better get rid of those sentimental, backward fancies as soon as possible. The East concerns itself very little about us, I can tell you! It can spare us."

She thrilled with pain at his words. "I should think you would be the last one to say so—you, who have so much treasure there."

"Will you please to understand," he said, turning upon her a face of bitter calmness, "that I claim no treasure anywhere—not even in heaven!"

She sat perfectly still, conscious that by some fatality of helpless incomprehension every word that she said goaded him, and she feared to speak again.

"Now I have hurt you," he said in his gentlest voice. "I am always hurting you. I oughtn't to come near you with my rough edges! I'll go away now, if you will tell me that you forgive me!"

She smiled at him without speaking, while her fair throat trembled with a pulse of pain.

"Will you let me take your hand a moment? It is so long since I have touched a woman's hand! God! how lonely I am! Don't look at me in that way; don't pity me, or I shall lose what little manhood I have left!"

"What is it?" she said, leaning towards him. "There is something strange in your face. If you are in trouble, tell me; it will help me to hear it. I am not so very happy myself."

"Why should I add my load to yours? I seem always to impose myself upon you, first my hopes, and now my—no, it isn't despair; it is only a kind of brutal numbness. You must have the fatal gift of sympathy, or you would never have seen my little hurt."

Miss Frances was not strong enough to bear the look in his eyes as he turned them upon her, with a dreary smile. She covered her face with one hand, while she whispered—

"Is it—you have not lost her?"

"Yes! Or, rather, I never had her. I've been dreaming like a boy all these years—'In sleep a king, but waking, no such matter.'"

"It is not death, then?"

"No, she is not dead. She is not even false; that is, not very false. How can I tell you how little it is, and yet how much! She is only a trifle selfish. Why shouldn't she be? Why should we men claim the exclusive right to choose the best for ourselves? It was selfish of me to ask her to share such a life as mine; and she has gently and reasonably reminded me that I'm not worth the sacrifice. It's quite true. I always knew I wasn't. She put it very delicately and sweetly;—she's the sweetest girl you ever saw. She'd marry me tomorrow if I could add myself, such as I am—she doesn't overrate me—to what she has already; but an exchange she wasn't prepared for. In all my life I never was so clearly estimated, body and soul. I don't blame her, you understand. When I left her, three years ago, I saw my way easily enough to a reputation, and an income, and a home in the East; she never thought of anything else; I never taught her to look for anything else. I dare say she rather enjoyed having a lover working for her in the unknown West; she enjoyed the pretty letters she wrote me; but when it came to the bare bones of existence in a mining camp, with a husband not very rich or very distinguished, she had nothing to clothe them with. You said once that to be happy here a woman must not have too much imagination; she hadn't quite enough. I had to be dead honest with her when I asked her to come. I told her there was nothing here but the mountains and the sunsets, and a few items of picturesqueness which count with some people. Of course I had to tell her I was but little better off than when I left. A man's experience is something he cannot set forth at its value to himself; she passed it over as a word of no practical meaning. There her imagination failed her again. She took me frankly at my own estimate; and in justice to her I must say I put myself at the lowest figures. I made a very poor show on paper."

"You wrote to her!" exclaimed Miss Frances. "You did not go on? Oh, you have made a great mistake! Do go: it cannot be too late. Letters are the most untrusty things!"

"Wait," he said. "There is something else. She has a head for business; she proposed that I should come East, and accept a superintendentship from a cousin of hers, the owner of a gun-factory in one of those shady New England towns women are so fond of. She intimated that he was in politics, this cousin, and of course would expect his employees to become part of his constituency. It's a very pretty little bribe, you see; when you add the—the girl, it's enough to shake a man—who wants that girl. I'm not worth much to myself, or to anybody else, apparently, but by Heaven I'll not sell out as cheap as that!

"It all amounts to nothing except one more illusion gone. If there is a woman on this earth that can love a man without knowing for what, and take the chances of life with him without counting the cost, I have never known her. I asked you once if a woman could do that. You hadn't the courage to tell me the truth. I wouldn't have been satisfied if you had; but I'm satisfied now."

"I believed she would be happy; I believe she would be, now, if only you would go to her and persuade her to try."

"I persuade her! I would never try to persuade a woman to be my wife were I dying for love of her! I don't think myself invented by nature to promote the happiness of woman, in the aggregate or singly. I know there are men who do: let them urge their claims. I thought that she loved me; that was another illusion. She will probably marry the cousin, and become the most loyal of his constituents. He is welcome to her; but there's a ghostly blank somewhere. How I have tired you! You'll be in bed another week for this selfishness of mine." He stopped, while a sudden thought brought a change to his face. "But when are you going home?"

"I cannot go," she said. Her weakness came over her like a cloud, darkening the room and pressing upon her heavily. "Will you give me your arm?"

At the stairs she stopped, and leaning against the wall looked at him with wide, hopeless eyes.

"We are cut off from everything. My friend does not need me now; she has gone home—alone. She is dead!"

Arnold took a long walk upon the hills that night, and smoked a great many cigars in gloomy meditation. He was thinking of two girls, as young men who smoke a great many cigars without counting them often are; he was also thinking of Arizona. He had fully made up his mind to resign, and depart for that problematic region as soon as his place was filled; but an alternative had presented itself to him with a pensive attractiveness—an alternative unmistakably associated with the fact that the schoolmistress was to remain in her present isolated circumstances. It even had occurred to him that there might be some question of duty involved in his "standing by her," as he phrased it to himself, "till she got her color back." There was an unconscious appeal in the last words he had heard her speak which constrained him to do so. He was not in the habit of pitying himself, but had there been another soul to follow this mental readjustment of himself to his mutilated life, it would surely have pitied the eagerness with which he clung to this one shadow of a duty to a fellow-creature. It was the measure of his loneliness.

It was late in November. The rains had begun again with sound and fury; with ranks of clouds forming along the mountain sides, and driven before the sea-winds upward through the gulches; with days of breeze and sunshine, when the fog veil was lightly lifted and blown apart, showing the valley always greener; with days of lowering stillness, when the veil descended and left the mountains alone, like islands of shadow rising from a sea of misty whiteness.

On such a lowering day, Miss Frances stood at the junction of three trails, in front of the door of the blacksmith's shop. She was wrapped in a dark blue cloak, with the hood drawn over her head; the cool dampness had given to her cheeks a clear, pure glow, and her brown eyes looked out with a cheerful light. She was watching the parting of the mist in the valley below; for a wind had sprung up, and now the rift widened, as the windows of heaven might have opened, giving a glimpse of the world to the "Blessed Damozel." All was dark above and around her; only a single shaft of sun-light pierced the fog, and startled into life a hundred tints of brightness in the valley. She caught the sparkle on the roofs and windows of the town ten miles away; the fields of sunburnt stubble glowed a deep Indian red; the young crops were tenderest emerald; and the line of the distant bay, a steel-blue thread against the horizon.

Arnold was plodding up the lower trail on his gray mare, fetlock deep in mud. He dismounted at the door of the shop, and called to him a small Mexican lad with a cheek of the tint of ripe corn.

"Here, Pedro Segundo! Take this mare up to the camp! Can you catch?" He tossed him a coin. "Bueno!"

"Mucho bueno!" said Pedro the First, looking on approvingly from the door of his shop.

Arnold turned to the schoolmistress, who was smiling from her perch on a pile of wet logs.

"I'm perfectly happy!" she said. "This east wind takes me home. I hear the bluebirds, and smell the salt-marshes and the wood-mosses. I'm not sure but that when the fog lifts we shall see white caps in the valley."

"I dare say there are some very good people down there," said Arnold, with deliberation, "but all the same I should welcome an inundation. Think what a climate this would be, if we could have the sea below us, knocking against the rocks on still nights, and thundering at us in a storm!"

"Don't speak of it! It makes me long for a miracle, or a judgment, or something that's not likely to happen."

"Meantime, I want you to come down the trail, and pass judgment on my bachelor quarters. I can't stand the boarding-house any longer! By Jove, I'm like the British footman in *Punch*—'what with them legs o' mutton and legs o' pork, I'm a'most wore out! I want a new hanimal inwented!' I've found an old girl down in the valley who consents to look after me and vary the monotony of my dinners at the highest market price. She isn't here yet, but the cabin is about ready. I want you to come down and look it over. I'm a perfect barbarian about color! You can't put it on too thick and strong to suit me. I dare say I need toning down."

They were slipping and sliding down the muddy trail, brushing the raindrops from the live-oak scrub as they passed. A subtle underlying content had lulled them both, of late, into an easier companionship than they had ever found possible before, and they were gay with that enjoyment of wet weather which is like an intoxication after seven months of drought.

"Now I suppose you like soft, harmonious tints and neutral effects. You're a bit of a conservative in everything, I fear."

"I think I should like plenty of color here, or else positive white; the monotony of the landscape and its own deep, low tones demand it. A neutral house would fade into an ash heap under this sun."

"Good! Then you'll like my dark little den, with its barbaric reds and blues."

They were at the gate of the little cottage, overlooking the valley. The gleam of sunlight had faded and the fog curtain rolled back. The house did indeed seem very dark as they entered. It was only a little after four o'clock, but the cloudy twilight of a short November day was suddenly descending upon them. The schoolmistress looked shyly around, while Arnold tramped about the rooms and sprung the shades up as high as they would go.

They were in a small, irregular parlor, wainscoted and floored in redwood, and lightly furnished with bamboo. This room communicated by a low arch with the dining-room beyond.

"I have some flags and spurs and old trophies to hang up there," he said, pointing to the arch; "and perhaps I can get you to sew the rings on the curtain that's to hang underneath. I don't want too much of the society of my angel from the valley, you know; besides, I want to shield her from the vulgar gaze, as they do the picture of the Madonna."

"It will serve you right if she never comes at all!"

"Oh, she's pining to come. She's dying to sacrifice herself for twenty-five dollars a month. Did I tell you, by the way, that I've had a rise in my salary? There is a rise in the work, too, which rather overbalances the increase of pay, but that's understood; for a good many years it will be more work than wage, but at the other end I hope it will be more wage than work. You don't seem to be very much interested in my affairs; if you knew how seldom I speak of them to any one but yourself, you might perhaps deign to listen."

"I am listening; but I'm thinking, too, that it's getting very late."

"See, here is my curtain!" he said, dragging out a breadth of heavy stuff. He took it to the window, and threw it over a Chinese lounge that stood beneath. "It's an old serape I picked up at Guadalajara five years ago:

the beauty of having a house is that all the old rubbish you have bored yourself with for years immediately becomes respectable and useful. I expect to become so myself. You don't say that you like my curtain!"

"I think it is very pagan looking, and rather—dirty."

"Well, I shan't make a point of the dirt. I dare say the thing would look just as well if it was clean. Won't you try my lounge?" he said, as she looked restlessly towards the door. "It was invented by a race that can loaf more naturally than we do: it takes an American back some time to relax enough to appreciate it."

Miss Frances half reluctantly drew her cloak about her, and yielded her Northern slenderness to the long Oriental undulations of the couch. Her head was thrown back, showing her fair throat and the sweet upward curves of her lips and brows.

Arnold gazed at her with too evident delight.

"Why won't you sit still? You cannot deny that you have never been so comfortable in your life before."

"It's a very good place to 'loaf and invite one's soul,'" she said, rising to a sitting position; "but that isn't my occupation at present. I must go home. It is almost dark."

"There is no hurry. I'm going with you. I want you to see how the little room lights up. I've never seen it by firelight, and I'll have my house-warming tonight!"

"Oh no, indeed! I must go back. There's the five o'clock whistle, now!"

"Well, we've an hour yet. You must get warm before you go."

He went out, and quickly returned with an armful of wood and shavings, which he crammed into the cold fireplace.

"What a litter you have made! Do you think your mature angel from the valley will stand that sort of thing?"

As she spoke, the rain descended in violence, sweeping across the piazza, and obliterating the fast-fading landscape. They could scarcely see each other in the darkness, and the trampling on the roof overhead made speech a useless effort. Almost as suddenly as it had opened upon them the tumult ceased, and in the silence that followed they listened to the heavy raindrops spattering from the eaves.

Arnold crossed to the window, where Miss Frances stood shivering and silent, with her hands clasped before her.

"I want you to light my fire," he said, with a certain concentration in his voice.

"Why do you not light it yourself?" She drew away from his out-stretched hand. "It seems to me you are a bit of a tyrant in your own house."

He drew a match across his knee and held it towards her: by its gleam she saw his pale, unsmiling face, and again that darkening of the eyes which she remembered.

"Do you refuse me such a little thing—my first guest? I ask it as a most especial grace!"

She took the match, and knelt with it in her hands; but it only flick-ered a moment, and went out. "It will not go for me. You must light it your-self."

He knelt beside her and struck another match. "We will try together," he said, placing it in her fingers and closing his hand about them. He held the trembling fingers and the little spark they guarded steadily against the shaving. It kindled; the flame breathed and brightened and curled upward among the crooked manzanita stumps, illuminating the two entranced young faces bending before it. Miss Frances rose to her feet, and Arnold, rising too, looked at her with a growing dread and longing in his eyes.

"You said today that you were happy, because in fancy you were at home. Is that the only happiness possible to you here?"

"I am quite contented here," she said. "I am getting acclimated."

"Oh, don't be content: I am not; I am horribly otherwise. I want something—so much that I dare not ask for it. You know what it is—Frances!"

"You said once that I reminded you—of her: is that the reason you—Am I consoling you?"

"Good God! I don't want consolation! *That* thing never existed; but here is the reality; I cannot part with it. I wish you had as little as I have, outside of this room where we two stand together!"

"I don't know that I have anything," she said under her breath.

"Then," said he, taking her in his arms, "I don't see but that we are ready to enter the kingdom of heaven. It seems very near to me."

They are still in exile: they have joined the band of lotus-eaters who inhabit that region of the West which is pervaded by a subtle breath from the Orient, blowing across the seas between. Mrs. Arnold has not yet made that first visit East which is said by her Californian friends to be so disillu-sioning, and the old home still hovers, like a beautiful mirage, on the receding horizon.

FRIEND BARTON'S "CONCERN"

It had been "borne in" upon him, more or less, during the long winter; it had not relaxed when the frosts unlocked their hold and the streams were set free from their long winter's silence, among the hills. He grew restless and abstracted under "the turnings of the Lord's hand upon him," and his speech unconsciously shaped itself into the Biblical cadences which came to him in his moments of spiritual exercise.

The bedrabbled snows of March shrank away before the keen, quickening sunbeams; the hills emerged, brown and sodden, like the chrysalis of the new year; the streams woke in a tumult, and all day and night their voices called from the hills back of the mill: the waste-weir was a foaming torrent, and spread itself in muddy shallows across the meadow, beyond the old garden where the robins and bluebirds were house-hunting. Friend Barton's trouble stirred with the life-blood of the year, and pressed upon him sorely; but as yet he gave it no words. He plodded about, among his lean kine, tempering the winds of March to his untimely lambs, and reconciling unnatural ewes to their maternal duties.

Friend Barton had never heard of the doctrine of the survival of the fittest, though it was the spring of 1812, and England and America were investigating the subject on the seas, while the nations of Europe were practically illustrating it. The "hospital tent," as the boys called an old corn-basket, covered with carpet, which stood beside the kitchen chimney, was seldom without an occupant—a brood of chilled chickens, a weakly lamb, or a wee pig (with too much blue in its pinkness), that had been left behind by its stouter brethren in the race for existence. The old mill hummed away through the day, and often late into the evening if time pressed, upon the grists which added a thin, intermittent stream of tribute to the family income. Whenever work was "slack," Friend Barton was sawing or chopping in the woodshed adjoining the kitchen; every moment he could seize or make he was there, stooping over the rapidly growing pile.

"Seems to me, father, thee's in a great hurry with the wood this spring. I don't know when we've had such a pile ahead."

"'T won't burn up any faster for being chopped," Friend Barton said; and then his wife Rachel knew that if he had a reason for being "fore-handed" with the wood, he was not ready to give it.

One rainy April afternoon, when the smoky gray distances began to take a tinge of green, and through the drip and rustle of the rain the call of the robins sounded, Friend Barton sat in the door of the barn, oiling the road-harness. The old chaise had been wheeled out and greased, and its cushions beaten and dusted.

An ox-team with a load of grain creaked up the hill and stopped at the mill door. The driver, seeing Friend Barton's broad-brimmed drab felt hat against the dark interior of the barn, came down the short lane leading from the mill, past the house and farm-buildings.

"Fixin' up for travelin', Uncle Tommy?"

Vain compliments, such as worldly titles of Mr. and Mrs., were unacceptable to Thomas Barton, and he was generally known and addressed as "Uncle Tommy" by the world's people of a younger generation.

"It is not in man that walketh to direct his own steps, neighbor Jordan. I am getting myself in readiness to obey the Lord, whichever way He shall call me."

Farmer Jordan cast a shrewd eye over the premises. They wore that patient, sad, exhumed look which old farm-buildings are apt to have in early spring. The roofs were black with rain, and brightened with patches of green moss. Farmer Jordan instinctively calculated how many "bunches o' shingle" would be required to rescue them from the decline into which they had fallen, indicated by these hectic green spots.

"Wal, the Lord calls most of us to stay at home and look after things, such weather as this. Good plantin' weather; good weather for breakin' ground; fust-rate weather for millin'! This is a reg'lar miller's rain, Uncle Tommy. You'd ought to be takin' advantage of it. I've got a grist back here; wish ye could manage to let me have it when I come back from store."

The grist was ground and delivered before Friend Barton went in to his supper that night. Dorothy Barton had been mixing bread, and was wiping her white arms and hands on the roller towel by the kitchen door, as her father stamped and scraped his feet on the stones outside.

"There! I do believe I forgot to toll neighbor Jordan's rye," he said, as he gave a final rub on the broom Dorothy handed out to him. "It's wonderful how careless I get!"

"Well, father, I don't suppose thee'd ever forget, and toll a grist twice!"

"I believe I've been mostly preserved from mistakes of that kind," said Friend Barton gently. "Well, well! To be sure," he continued musingly. "It may be the Lord who stays my hand from gathering profit unto myself while his lambs go unfed."

Dorothy put her hands on her father's shoulders: she was almost as tall as he, and could look into his patient, troubled eyes.

"Father, I know what thee is thinking of, but do think long. It will be a hard year; the boys ought to go to school; and mother is so feeble!"

Friend Barton's "concern" kept him awake that night. His wife watched by his side, giving no sign, lest her wakeful presence should disturb his silent wrestlings. The tall, cherry-wood clock in the entry measured the hours, as they passed, with its slow, dispassionate tick.

At two o'clock Rachel Barton was awakened from her first sleep of weariness by her husband's voice, whispering heavily in the darkness.

"My way is hedged up! I see no way to go forward. Lord, strengthen my patience, that I murmur not, after all I have seen of thy goodness. I find daily bread is very desirable; want and necessity are painful to nature; but shall I follow Thee for the sake of the loaves, or will it do to forsake Thee in times of emptiness and abasement?"

There was silence again, and restless tossings and sighings continued the struggle.

"Thomas," the wife's voice spoke tremulously in the darkness, "my dear husband, I know whither thy thoughts are tending. If the Spirit is with thee, do not deny it for our sakes, I pray thee. The Lord did not give thee thy wife and children to hang as a millstone round thy neck. I am thy helpmeet, to strengthen thee in his service. I am thankful that I have my health this spring better than usual, and Dorothy is a wonderful help. Her spirit was sent to sustain me in thy long absences. Go, dear, and serve our Master, who has called thee in these bitter strivings! Dorothy and I will keep things together as well as we can. The way will open—never fear!" She put out her hand and touched his face in the darkness; there were tears on the furrowed cheeks. "Try to sleep, dear, and let thy spirit have rest. There is but one answer to this call."

With the first drowsy twitterings of the birds, when the crescent-shaped openings in the board shutters began to define themselves clearly in the shadowy room, they arose and went about their morning tasks in silence. Friend Barton's step was a little heavier than usual, and the hollows round his wife's pale brown eyes were a little deeper. As he sat on the splint-bottomed chair by the kitchen fireplace, drawing on his boots, she placed her hands on his shoulders, and touched with her cheek the worn spot on the top of his head.

"Thee will lay this concern before meeting tomorrow, father?"

"I had it on my mind to do so—if my light be not quenched before then."

Friend Barton's light was not quenched. Words came to him, without seeking—a sure sign that the Spirit was with him—in which to "open the concern" that had ripened in his mind, of a religious visit to the meeting constituting the yearly meetings of Philadelphia and Baltimore. A "minute" was given him, encouraging him in the name, and with the full concurrence, of the monthly meetings of Nine Partners and Stony Valley, to go wherever the Truth might lead him.

While Friend Barton was thus freshly anointed, and "abundantly encouraged," his wife, Rachel, was talking with Dorothy, in the low upper chamber known as the "wheel-room."

Dorothy was spinning wool on the big wheel, dressed in her light calico short gown and brown quilted petticoat; her arms were bare, and her hair was gathered away from her flushed cheeks and knotted behind her ears. The roof sloped down on one side, and the light came from a long, low window under the eaves. There was another window (shaped like a half-moon, high up in the peak), but it sent down only one long beam of sunlight, which glimmered across the dust and fell upon Dorothy's white neck.

The wheel was humming a quick measure and Dorothy trod lightly back and forth, the wheel-pin in one hand, the other holding the tense, lengthening thread, which the spindle devoured again.

"Dorothy, thee looks warm: can't thee sit down a moment, while I talk to thee?"

"Is it anything important, mother? I want to get my twenty knots before dinner." She paused as she joined a long tress of wool at the spindle. "Is it anything about father?"

"Yes, it's about father, and all of us."

"I know," said Dorothy, with a sigh. "He's going away again!"

"Yes, dear. He feels that he is called. It is a time of trouble and contention everywhere: 'the harvest,' truly, 'is plenteous, but the laborers are few.'"

"There are not so many 'laborers' here, mother, though to be sure, the harvest—"

"Dorothy, my daughter, don't let a spirit of levity creep into thy speech. Thy father has striven and wrestled with his urgings. I've seen it working on him all winter. He feels, now, it is the Lord's will."

"I don't see how he can be so sure," said Dorothy, swaying gloomily to and fro against the wheel. "I don't care for myself, I'm not afraid of work, but thee's not able to do what thee does now, mother. If I have outside things to look after, how can I help thee as I should? And the boys are about as much dependence as a flock of barn swallows!"

"Don't thee fret about me, dear; the way will open. Thy father has thought and planned for us. Have patience while I tell thee. Thee knows that Walter Evesham's pond is small and his mill is doing a thriving business?"

"Yes, indeed, I know it!" Dorothy exclaimed. "He has his own share, and ours too, most of it!"

"Wait, dear, wait! Thy father has rented him the ponds, to use when his own gives out. He is to have the control of the water, and it will give us a little income, even though the old mill does stand idle."

"He may as well take the mill, too. If father is away all summer it will be useless ever to start it again. Thee'll see, mother, how it will end, if Walter Evesham has the custom and the water all summer. I think it's miserable for a young man to be so keen about money."

"Dorothy, seems to me thee's hasty in thy judgments. I never heard that said of Walter Evesham. His father left him with capital to improve his mill. It does better work than ours; we can't complain of that. Thy father was never one to study much after ways of making money. He felt he had no right to more than an honest livelihood. I don't say that Walter Evesham's in the wrong. We know that Joseph took advantage of his opportunities, though I can't say that I ever felt much unity with some of his transactions. What would thee have, my dear? Thee's discouraged with thy father for choosing the thorny way, which we tread with him; but thee seems no better satisfied with one who considers the flesh and its wants'"

"I don't know, mother, what I want for myself; that doesn't matter; but for thee I would have rest from all these cruel worries thee has borne so long."

She buried her face in her mother's lap and put her strong young arms about the frail, toil-bent form.

"There, there, dear. Try to rule thy spirit, Dorothy. Thee's too much worked up about this. They are not worries to me. I am thankful we have nothing to decide one way or the other, only to do our best with what is given us. Thee's not thyself, dear. Go downstairs and fetch in the clothes, and don't hurry; stay out till thee gets more composed."

Dorothy did not succeed in bringing herself into unity with her father's call, but she came to a fuller realization of his struggle. When he bade them good-by his face showed what it had cost him; but Rachel was calm and cheerful. The pain of parting is keenest to those who go, but it stays longer with those that are left behind.

"Dorothy, take good care of thy mother!" Friend Barton said, taking his daughter's face between his hands and gravely kissing her brow between the low-parted ripples of her hair.

"Yes, father," she said, looking into his eyes; "Thee knows I'm thy eldest son."

They watched the old chaise swing round the corner of the lane, then the pollard willows shut it from sight.

"Come, mother," said Dorothy, hurrying her in at the gate. "I'm going to make a great pot of mush, and have it hot for supper, and fried for breakfast, and warmed up with molasses for dinner, and there'll be some cold with milk for supper, and we shan't have any cooking to do at all!"

They went around by the kitchen door. Rachel stopped in the wood-shed, and the tears rushed to her eyes.

"Dear father! How he has worked over that wood, early and late, to spare us!"

We will not revive Dorothy's struggles with the farm-work, and with the boys. They were an isolated family at the mill-house; their peculiar faith isolated them still more, and they were twelve miles from meeting and the settlement of Friends at Stony Valley. Dorothy's pride kept her silent about her needs, lest they might bring reproach upon her father among the neighbors, who would not be likely to feel the urgency of his spiritual summons.

The summer heats came on apace and the nights grew shorter. It seemed to Dorothy that she had hardly stretched out her tired young body and forgotten her cares, in the low, attic bedroom, before the east was streaked with light and the birds were singing in the apple-trees, whose falling blossoms drifted in at the window.

One day in early June, Friend Barton's flock of sheep (consisting of nine experienced ewes, six yearlings, and a sprinkling of close-curled lambs whose legs had not yet come into mature relations with their bodies) was gathered in a wattled inclosure, beside the stream that flowed into the mill-head. It was supplied by the waste from the pond, and, when the gate was shut, rambled easily over the gray slate pebbles, with here and there a fall just forcible enough to serve as a douche-bath for a well-grown sheep. The victims were panting in their heavy fleeces, and mingling their hoarse, plaintive tremolo with the ripple of the water and the sound of young voices in a frolic. Dorothy had divided her forces for the washing to the best advantage. The two elder boys stood in midstream to receive the sheep, which she, with the help of little Jimmy, caught and dragged to the bank.

The boys were at work now upon an elderly ewe, while Dorothy stood on the brink of the stream braced against an ash sapling, dragging forward by the fleece a beautiful but reluctant yearling. Her bare feet were incased in a pair of moccasins that laced around the ankle; her petticoats were kilted, and her broad hat bound down with a ribbon; one sleeve was rolled up, the other had been sacrificed in a scuffle in the sheep-pen. The new candidate for immersion stood bleating and trembling with her forefeet planted against the slippery bank, pushing back with all her strength while Jimmy propelled from the rear.

"Boys!" Dorothy's clear voice called across the stream. "*Do* hurry! She's been in long enough, now! Keep her head up, can't you, and squeeze the wool *hard*! You're not *half* washing! Oh, Reuby! thee'll drown her! Keep her *head* up!"

Another unlucky douse and another half-smothered bleat—Dorothy released the yearling and plunged to the rescue. "Go after that lamb, Reuby!" she cried with exasperation in her voice. Reuby followed the yearling, that had disappeared over the orchard slope, upsetting an obstacle in its path, which happened to be Jimmy. He was wailing now on the bank, while Dorothy, with the ewe's nose tucked comfortably in the bend of her arm, was parting and squeezing the fleece, with the water swirling round her. Her stout arms ached, and her ears were stunned with the incessant bleatings; she counted with dismay the sheep still waiting in the pen. "Oh, Jimmy! Do stop crying, or else go to the house!"

"He'd better go after Reuby," said Sheppard Barton, who was now Dorothy's sole dependence.

"Oh yes, do, Jimmy, that's a good boy. Tell him to let the yearling go and come back quick."

The water had run low that morning in Evesham's pond. He shut down the mill, and strode up the hills, across lots, to raise the gate of the lower Barton pond, which had been heading up for his use. He passed the cornfield where, a month before, he had seen pretty Dorothy Barton dropping corn with her brothers. It made him ache to think of Dorothy with her feeble mother, the boys as wild as preachers' sons proverbially are, and the old farm running down on her hands; the fences all needed mending, and there went Reuben Barton, now, careering over the fields in chase of a stray yearling. His mother's house was big, and lonely, and empty; and he flushed as he thought of the "one ewe-lamb" he coveted out of Friend Barton's rugged pastures.

As Evesham raised the gate, and leaned to watch the water swirl and gurgle through the "trunk," sucking the long weeds with it, and thickening with its tumult the clear current of the stream, the sound of voices and the bleating of sheep came up from below. He had not the farming instincts in his blood; the distant bleating, the hot June sunshine and cloudless sky did not suggest to him sheep-washing; but now came a boy's voice shouting and a cry of distress, and he remembered with a thrill that Friend Barton used the stream for that peaceful purpose. He shut down the gate and tore along through the ferns and tangled grass till he came to the sheep-pen, where the bank was muddy and trampled. The prisoners were bleating drearily and looking with longing eyes across to the other side, where those who had suffered were now straying and cropping the short turf through the lights and shadows of the orchard.

There was no other sign of life, except a broad hat with a brown ribbon buffeted about in an eddy among the stones. The stream dipped now below the hill, and the current, still racing fast with the impetus he had given it, shot away amongst the hazel thickets that crowded close to the brink. He was obliged to make a detour by the orchard and to come out below at the "mill-head," a black, deep pool with an ugly ripple setting across it to the head-gate. He saw something white clinging there, and ran round the brink. It was the sodden fleece of the old ewe, which had been drifted against the head-gate and held there to her death. Evesham, with a sickening contraction of the heart, threw off his jacket for a plunge, when Dorothy's voice called rather faintly from the willows on the opposite bank.

"Don't jump! I'm here," she said. Evesham searched the willows and found her seated in the sun, just beyond, half buried in a bed of ferns.

"I *shouldn't* have called thee," she said shyly, as he sank pale and panting beside her, "but thee looked—I thought thee was going to jump into the mill-head!"

"I thought *you* were there, Dorothy!"

"I was there quite long enough. Shep pulled me out; I was too tired to help myself much." Dorothy held her palm pressed against her temple and the blood trickled from beneath, streaking her pale, wet cheek.

"He's gone to the house to get me a cloak. I don't want mother to see me, not yet," she said.

"I'm afraid you ought not to wait, Dorothy. Let me take you to the house, won't you? I'm afraid you'll get a deadly chill."

Dorothy did not look in the least like death. She was blushing now, because Evesham would think it so strange of her to stay, and yet she could not rise in her wet clothes, that clung to her like the calyx to a bud.

"Let me see that cut, Dorothy!"

"Oh, it's nothing. I don't wish thee to look at it!"

"But I will! Do you want to make me your murderer, sitting there in your wet clothes with a cut on your head?"

He drew away her hand; the wound, indeed, was no great affair, but he bound it up deftly with strips of his handkerchief. Dorothy's wet curls touched his fingers and clung to them, and her eyelashes drooped lower and lower.

"I think it was *very* stupid of thee. Didn't thee hear us from the dam? I'm sure we made noise enough."

"Yes, I heard you when it was too late. I heard the sheep before, but how could I imagine that you, Dorothy, and three boys as big as cockerels, were sheep-washing? It's the most preposterous thing I ever heard of!",

"Well, I can't help being a woman, and the sheep had to be washed. I think there ought to be more men in the world when half of them are preaching and fighting."

"If you'd only let the men who are left help you a little, Dorothy."

"I don't want any help. I only *don't* want to be washed into the mill-head."

They both laughed, and Evesham began again entreating her to let him take her to the house.

"Hasn't thee a coat or something I could put around me until Shep comes?" said Dorothy. "He must be here soon."

"Yes, I've a jacket here somewhere."

He sped away to find it, and faithless Dorothy, as the willows closed between them, sprang to her feet and fled like a startled Naiad to the house.

When Evesham, pushing through the willows, saw nothing but the bed of wet, crushed ferns and the trail through the long grass where Dorothy's feet had fled, he smiled grimly to himself, remembering that "ewe-lambs" are not always as meek as they look.

That evening Rachel had received a letter from Friend Barton and was preparing to read it aloud to the children. They were in the kitchen, where the boys had been helping Dorothy in a desultory manner to shell corn for the chickens; but now all was silence while Rachel wiped her glasses and turned the large sheet of paper, squared with many foldings, to the candle.

She read the date, " 'London Grove, 5th month, 22d.—Most affectionately beloved.' "

"He means us all," said Rachel, turning to the children with a tender smile. "It's spelled with a small *b*."

"He means thee!" said Dorothy, laughing. "Thee's not such a very big beloved."

There was a moment's silence. "I don't know that the opening of the letter is of general interest," Rachel mused, with her eyes traveling slowly down the page. "He says: 'In regard to my health, lest thee should concern thyself, I am thankful to say I have never enjoyed better since years have made me acquainted with my infirmities of body, and I earnestly hope that my dear wife and children are enjoying the same blessing.

"'I trust the boys are not deficient in obedience and helpfulness. At Sheppard's age I had already begun to take the duties of a man upon my shoulders.'"

Sheppard giggled uncomfortably, and Dorothy laughed outright.

"Oh, if father only *knew* how good the boys are! Mother, thee must write and tell him about their 'helpfulness and obedience'! Thee can tell him their appetites keep up pretty well; they manage to take their meals regularly, and they are *always* out of bed by eight o'clock to help me hang up the milking-stool!"

"Just wait till thee gets into the mill-head again, Dorothy Barton! Thee needn't come to *me* to help thee out!"

"Go on, mother. Don't let the boys interrupt thee!"

"Well," said Rachel, rousing herself, "where was I? Oh, 'At Sheppard's age'! Well, next come some allusions to the places where he has visited and his spiritual exercises there. I don't know that the boys are quite old enough to enter into this yet. Thee'd better read it thyself, Dorothy. I'm keeping all father's letters for the boys to read when they are old enough to appreciate them."

"Well, I think thee might read to us about where he's been preachin'. We can understand a great deal more than thee thinks we can," said Shep in an injured voice. "Reuby can preach some himself. Thee ought to hear him, mother. It's almost as good as meetin'."

"I *wondered* how Reuby spent his time," said Dorothy, and the mother hastened to interpose.

"Well! here's a passage that may be interesting: 'On sixth day attended the youths' meeting here, a pretty favored time on the whole. Joseph' (that's Joseph Carpenter; he mentions him aways back) 'had good service in lively testimony, while I was calm and easy without a word to say. At a meeting at Plumstead we suffered long, but at length we felt relieved. The unfaithful were admonished, the youth invited, and the heavy-hearted encouraged. It was a heavenly time.' Heretofore he seems to have been closed up with silence a good deal, but now the way opens continually for him to free himself. He's been 'much favored,' he says, 'of late.' Reuby, what's thee doing to thy brothers?" (Shep and Reuby, who had been persecuting Jimmy by pouring handfuls of corn down the neck of his jacket until he had taken refuge behind Dorothy's chair, were now recriminating with corn-cobs on each other's faces.) "Dorothy, can't thee keep those boys quiet?"

"Did thee ever know them to be quiet?" said Dorothy, helping Jimmy to relieve himself of his corn.

"Well now, listen." Rachel continued placidly, " 'Second day, 27th' (of fifth month, he means; the letter's been a long time coming), 'attended their mid-week meeting at London Grove, where my tongue, as it were, clave to the roof of my mouth, while Hannah Husbands was much favored and enabled to lift up her voice like the song of an angel'–"

"Who's Hannah Husbands?" Dorothy interrupted.

"Thee doesn't know her, dear. She was second cousin to thy father's stepmother; the families were not congenial, I believe, but she has a great gift for the ministry."

"I should think she'd better be at home with her children, if she has any. Fancy *thee*, mother, going about to strange meetings and lifting up thy voice—"

"Hush, hush, Dorothy! Thy tongue's running away with thee. Consider the example thee's setting the boys."

"Thee'd better write to father about Dorothy, mother. Perhaps Hannah Husbands would like to know what she thinks about her preachin'."

"Well, now, be quiet, all of you. Here's something about Dorothy: 'I know that my dear daughter Dorothy is faithful and loving, albeit somewhat quick of speech and restive under obligation. I would have thee remind her that an unwillingness to accept help from others argues a want of Christian Meekness. Entreat her from me not to conceal her needs from our neighbors, if so be she find her work oppressive. We know them to be of kindly intention, though not of our way of thinking in all particulars. Let her receive help from them, not as individuals, but as instruments of the Lord's protection, which it were impiety and ingratitude to deny.' "

"There!" cried Shep. "That means thee is to let Luke Jordan finish the sheep-washing. Thee'd better have done it in the first place. We shouldn't have the old ewe to pick if thee had."

Dorothy was dimpling at the idea of Luke Jordan in the character of an instrument of heavenly protection. She had not regarded him in that light, it must be confessed, but had rejected him with scorn.

"He may, if he wants to," she said; "but you boys shall drive them over. I'll have nothing to do with it."

"And shear them too, Dorothy? He asked to shear them long ago."

"Well, *let* him shear them and keep the wool too."

"I wouldn't say that, Dorothy," said Rachel Barton. "We need the wool, and it seems as if over-payment might not be quite honest, either."

"Oh, mother, mother! What a mother thee is!" cried Dorothy laughing and rumpling Rachel's cap-strings in a tumultuous embrace.

"She's a great deal too good for *thee*, Dorothy Barton."

"She's too good for all of us. How did thee ever come to have such a graceless set of children, mother?"

"I'm very well satisfied," said Rachel. "But now do be quiet and let's finish the letter. We must get to bed some time tonight!"

*   *   *   *   *

The wild clematis was in blossom now; the fences were white with it, and the rusty cedars were crowned with virgin wreaths; but the weeds were thick in the garden and in the potato patch. Dorothy, stretching her cramped back, looked longingly up the shadowy vista of the farm-lane that had nothing to do but ramble off into the remotest green fields, where the daisies' faces were as white and clear as in early June.

One hot August night she came home late from the store. The stars were thick in the sky; the katydids made the night oppressive with their rasping questionings, and a hoarse revel of frogs kept the ponds from falling asleep in the shadow of the hills.

"Is thee very tired tonight, Dorothy?" her mother asked, as she took her seat on the low step of the porch. "Would thee mind turning old John out thyself?"

"No, mother, I'm not tired. But why? Oh, *I* know!" cried Dorothy with a quick laugh. "The dance at Slocum's barn. I thought those boys were uncommonly helpful."

"Yes, dear, it's but natural they should want to see it. Hark! we can hear the music from here."

They listened, and the breeze brought across the fields the sound of fiddles and the rhythmic tramp of feet, softened by the distance. Dorothy's young pulses leaped.

"Mother, is it any harm for them just to see it? They have so little fun, except what they get out of teasing and shirking."

"My dear, thy father would never countenance such a scene of frivolity, or permit one of his children to look upon it; through our eyes and ears the world takes possession of our hearts."

"Then I'm to spare the boys this temptation, mother? Thee will trust *me* to pass the barn?"

"I would trust my boys, if they were thy age, Dorothy; but their resolution is tender like their years."

It might be questioned whether the frame of mind in which the boys went to bed that night under their mother's eye, for Rachel could be firm in a case of conscience, was more improving than the frivolity of Slocum's barn.

"Mother," called Dorothy, looking in at the kitchen window where Rachel was stooping over the embers in the fireplace to light a bedroom candle, "I want to speak to thee."

Rachel came to the window, screening the candle with her hand.

"Will thee trust me to look at the dancing a little while? It is so very near."

"Why, Dorothy, does thee want to?"

"Yes, mother, I believe I do. I've never seen a dance in my life. It cannot ruin me to look just once."

Rachel stood puzzled.

"Thee's old enough to judge for thyself, Dorothy. But, my child, do not tamper with thy inclinations through heedless curiosity. Thee knows thee's more impulsive than I could wish for thy own peace."

"I'll be very careful, mother. If I feel in the least wicked I will come straight away."

She kissed her mother's hand that rested on the window-sill. Rachel did not like the kiss, nor Dorothy's brilliant eyes and flushed cheeks, as the candle revealed them like a fair picture painted on the darkness. She hesitated, but Dorothy sped away up the lane with old John lagging at his halter.

Was it the music growing nearer that quickened her breathing, or only the closeness of the night shut in between the wild grapevine curtains swung from one dark cedar column to another? She caught the sweetbrier's breath as she hurried by, and now a loop in the leafy curtain revealed the pond, lying black in a hollow of the hills with a whole heaven of stars reflected in it. Old John stumbled along over the stones, cropping the grass as he went. Dorothy tugged at his halter and urged him on to the head of the lane, where two farm-gates stood at right angles. One of them was open and a number of horses were tethered in a row along the fence within. They whinnied a cheerful greeting to John as Dorothy slipped his halter and shut him into the field adjoining. Now should she walk into temptation with her eyes and ears open? The gate stood wide, with only one field of perfumed meadow-grass between her and the lights and music of Slocum's barn. The sound of revelry by night could hardly have taken a more innocent form than this rustic dancing of neighbors after a "raisin' bee," but had it been the rout of Comus and his crew, and Dorothy the Lady Una trembling near, her heart could hardly have throbbed more quickly as she crossed the dewy meadow. A young maple stood within ten rods of the barn, and here she crouched in shadow.

The great doors stood wide open and lanterns were hung from the beams, lighting the space between the mows where a dance was set, with youths and maidens in two long rows. The fiddlers sat on barrel-heads near the door; a lantern hanging just behind projected their shadows across the square of light on the trodden space in front, where they executed a grotesque pantomime, keeping time to the music with spectral wavings and noddings. The dancers were Dorothy's young neighbors, whom she had known, and yet not known, all her life, but they had the strangeness of familiar faces seen suddenly in some fantastic dream.

Surely that was Nancy Slocum in the bright pink gown heading the line of girls, and that was Luke Jordan's sunburnt profile leaning from his place to pluck a straw from the mow behind him. They were marching, and the measured tramp of feet keeping solid time to the fiddles set a strange tumult vibrating in Dorothy's blood; and now it stopped, with a thrill, as she recognized that Evesham was there, marching with the young men, and that his peer was not among them. The perception of his difference came to her with a vivid shock. He was coming forward now with his light, firm step, formidable in evening dress and with a smile of subtle triumph in his eyes, to meet Nancy Slocum in the bright pink gown. Dorothy felt she hated pink of all the colors her faith had abjured. She could see, in spite of the obnoxious gown, that Nancy was very pretty. He was taking her first by the right hand, then by the left, and turning her gayly about; and now they were meeting again for the fourth or fifth time in the centre of the barn, with all eyes upon them, and the music lingered while Nancy, holding out her pink petticoats, coyly revolved around him. Then began a mysterious turning and clasping of hands, and weaving of Nancy's pink frock and Evesham's dark blue coat and white breeches in and out of the line of figures, until they met at the door, and, taking each other by both hands, swept with a joyous measure to the head of the barn. Dorothy gave a little choking sigh.

What a senseless whirl it was. She was thrilling with a new and strange excitement, too near the edge of pain to be long endured as a pleasure. If this were the influence of dancing she did not wonder so much at her father's scruples, and yet it held her like a spell.

All hands were lifted now, making an arch through which Evesham, holding Nancy by the hands, raced, stooping and laughing. As they emerged at the door, Evesham threw up his head to shake a brown lock back. He looked flushed and boyishly gay, and his hazel eye searched the darkness with that subtle ray of triumph in it which made Dorothy afraid. She drew back behind the tree and pressed her hot cheek to the cool, rough bark. She longed for the stillness of the starlit meadow, and the dim lane with its faint perfumes and whispering leaves.

But now suddenly the music stopped and the dance broke up in a tumult of voices. Dorothy stole backward in the shadow of the tree-trunk, until it joined the darkness of the meadow, and then fled, stumbling along with blinded eyes, the music still vibrating in her ears. Then came a quick rush of footsteps behind her, swishing through the long grass. She did not look back, but quickened her pace, struggling to reach the gate. Evesham was there before her. He had swung the gate to and was leaning with his back against it, laughing and panting.

"I've caught you, Dorothy, you little deceiver! You'll not get rid of me tonight with any of your tricks. I'm going to take you home to your mother and tell her you were peeping at the dancing."

"Mother knows that I came; I asked her," said Dorothy. Her knees were trembling and her heart almost choked her with its throbbing.

"I'm so glad you don't dance, Dorothy. This is much nicer than the barn, and the katydids are better fiddlers than old Darby and his son. I'll open the gate if you will put your hand in mine, so that I can be sure of you, you little runaway."

"I will stay here all night, first," said Dorothy, in a low, quivering voice.

"As you choose. I shall be happy as long as you are here."

Dead silence, while the katydids seemed to keep time to their heart-beats; the fiddles began tuning for another reel, and the horses, tethered near, stretched out their necks with low, inquiring whinnies.

"Dorothy," said Evesham softly, leaning toward her and trying to see her face in the darkness, "are you angry with me? Don't you think you deserve a little punishment for the trick you played me at the mill-head?"

"It was all thy fault for insisting." Dorothy was too excited and angry to cry, but she was as miserable as she had ever been in her life before. "I didn't want thee to stay. People that force themselves where they are not wanted must take what they get."

"What did you say, Dorothy?"

"I say I didn't want thee then. I do not want thee now. Thee may go back to thy fiddling and dancing. I'd rather have one of those dumb brutes for company tonight than thee, Walter Evesham."

"Very well; the reel has begun," said Evesham. "Fanny Jordan is waiting to dance it with me, or if she isn't she ought to be. Shall I open the gate for you?"

She passed out in silence, and the gate swung to with a heavy jar. She made good speed down the lane and then waited outside the fence till her breath came more quietly.

"Is that thee, Dorothy?" Rachel's voice called from the porch. She came out to meet her daughter and they went along the walk together. "How damp thy forehead is, child. Is the night so warm?" They sat down on the low steps and Dorothy slid her arm under her mother's and laid her soft palm against the one less soft by twenty years of toil for others. "Thee's not been long, dear; was it as much as thee expected?"

"Mother, it was dreadful! I never wish to hear a fiddle again as long as I live."

Rachel opened the way for Dorothy to speak further; she was not without some mild stirrings of curiosity on the subject herself, but Dorothy had no more to say.

They went into the house soon after, and as they separated for the night Dorothy clung to her mother with a little nervous laugh.

"Mother, what is that text about Ephraim?"

"Ephraim is joined to idols?" Rachel suggested.

"Yes, Ephraim is joined to his idols," said Dorothy, lifting her head. "Let him go!"

"Let him *alone*," corrected Rachel.

"Let him *alone!*" Dorothy repeated. "That is better yet."

"What's thee thinking of, dear?"

"Oh, I'm thinking about the dance in the barn."

"I'm glad thee looks at it in that light," said Rachel calmly.

*   *   *   *   *

Dorothy knelt by her bed in the low chamber under the eaves, crying to herself that she was not the child of her mother any more.

She felt that she had lost something, that in truth had never been hers. It was but the unconscious poise of her unawakened girlhood which had been stirred; she had mistaken it for that abiding peace which is not lost or won in a day.

Dorothy could no more stifle the spring thrills in her blood than she could crush the color out of her cheek or brush the ripples out of her bright hair, but she longed for the cool grays and the still waters. She prayed that the "grave and beautiful damsel called Discretion" might take her by the hand and lead her to that "upper chamber, whose name is Peace." She lay awake listening to the music from the barn, and waiting through breathless silences for it to begin again. She wondered if Fanny Jordan had grown any prettier since she had seen her as a half-grown girl, and then she despised herself for the thought. The katydids seemed to beat their wings upon her brain, and all the noises of the night, far and near, came to her strained senses as if her silent chamber were a whispering gallery. The clock struck twelve, and in the silence that followed she missed the music; but voices talking and laughing were coming down the lane. There was the clink of a horse's hoof on the stones: now it was lost on the turf, and now they were all trooping noisily past the house. She buried her head in her pillow and tried to bury with it the consciousness that she was wondering if Evesham were there laughing with the rest.

Yes, Evesham was there. He walked with Farmer Jordan, behind the young men and girls, and discussed with him, somewhat absently, the war news and the prices of grain.

As they passed the dark old house, spreading its wide roofs like a hen gathering her chickens under her wing, he became suddenly silent. A white curtain flapped in and out of an upper window. Evesham looked up and slightly raised his hat, but his instinct failed him there—it was the window of the boys' room.

"Queer kinks them old Friend preachers gits into their heads sometimes," said Farmer Jordan, as they passed the empty mill. "Now what do you s'pose took Uncle Tommy Barton off right on top of plantin', leavin' his wife 'n' critters 'n' child'en to look after themselves? Mighty good preachin' it ought to be to make up for such practicin'. Wonderful set ag'in the war, Uncle Tommy is. He's a-preachin' up peace now. But Lord! all the preachin' sense Moses won't keep men from fightin' when their blood's up and there's ter'tory in it."

"It makes saints of the women," said Evesham shortly.

"Wal, yes. Saints in heaven before their time, some of 'em. There's Dorothy, now. She'll hoe her row with any saint in the kingdom or out of it. I never see a hulsomer-lookin' gal. My Luke, he run the furrers in her corn-patch last May. Said it made him sick to see a gal like that a-staggerin' after a plough. She wouldn't more 'n half let him. She's a proud little piece. They're all proud, Quakers is. I never could see no 'poorness of spirit,' come to git at 'em. And they're wonderful clannish, too. My Luke, he'd a notion he'd like to run the hull concern, Dorothy 'n' all; but I told him he might's well p'int off. Them Quaker gals don't never marry out o' meetin'. Besides, the farm's too poor."

"Good-night, Mr. Jordan," said Evesham suddenly. "I'm off across lots." He leaped the fence, crashed through the alder hedgerow, and disappeared in the dusky meadow.

Evesham was by no means satisfied with his experiments in planetary distances. Somewhere, he felt sure, either in his orbit or hers, there must be a point where Dorothy would be less insensible to the attraction of atoms in the mass. Thus far she had reversed the laws of the spheres, and the greater had followed the less. When she had first begun to hold a permanent place in his thoughts he had invested her with something of that atmosphere of peace and cool passivity which hedges in the women of her faith. It had been like a thin, clear glass, revealing her loveliness, but cutting off the magnetic currents. A young man is not long satisfied with the mystery his thoughts have woven around the woman who is their object. Evesham had grown impatient; he had broken the spell of her sweet remoteness. He had touched her and found her human, deliciously, distractingly human, but with a streak of that obduracy which history has attributed to the Quakers under persecution. In vain he haunted the mill-dam, and bribed the boys with traps and pop-guns, and lingered at the well-curb to ask Dorothy for water that did not reach his thirst. She was there in the flesh, with her arms aloft balancing the well-sweep, while he stooped with his lips at the bucket; but in spirit she was unapproachable. He felt, with disgust at his own persistence, that she even grudged him the water. He grew savage and restless, and fretted over the subtle changes that he counted in Dorothy as the summer waned. She was thinner and paler; perhaps with the heats of harvest, which had not, indeed, been burdensome from its abundance. Her eyes were darker and shyer, and her voice more languid. Was she wearing down with all this work and care? A fierce disgust possessed him that this sweet life should be cast into the breach between faith and works.

He did not see that Rachel Barton had changed, too, with a change that meant more, at her age, than Dorothy's flushings and palings. He did not miss the mother's bent form from the garden, or the bench by the kitchen door where she had been used to wash the milk-things.

Dorothy washed the milk-things now, and the mother spent her days in the sunny east room, between her bed and the easy-chair, where she sat and mused for hours over the five letters that she had received from her husband in as many months. The boys had, in a measure, justified their father's faith in them, since Rachel's illness, and Dorothy was released from much of her out-door work; but the silence of the kitchen, when she was there alone with her ironing and dish washing, was a heavier burden than she had yet known.

Nature sometimes strikes in upon the hopeless monotony of life in remote farmhouses with one of her phenomenal moods. They come like besoms of destruction, but they scatter the web of stifling routine; they fling into the stiffening pool the stone which jars the atoms into crystal.

The storms, that had ambushed in the lurid August skies and circled ominously round the horizon during the first weeks of September, broke at last in an equinoctial which was long remembered in the mill-house. It took its place in the family calendar of momentous dates with the hard winter of 1800, with the late frost that had coated the incipient apples with ice and frozen the new potatoes in the ground in the spring of '97, and with the year the typhus had visited the valley.

The rain had been falling a night and a day; it had been welcomed with thanksgiving, but it had worn out its welcome some hours since, and now the early darkness was coming on without a lull in the storm. Dorothy and the two older boys had made the rounds of the farm-buildings, seeing all safe for the second night. The barns and mill stood on high ground, while the house occupied the sheltered hollow between. Little streams from the hills were washing in turbid currents across the lower levels; the waste-weir roared as in early spring, the garden was inundated, and the meadow a shallow pond. The sheep had been driven into the upper barn floor: the chickens were in the corn-bin; and old John and the cows had been transferred from the stable, that stood low, to the weighing floor of the mill. A gloomy echoing and gurgling sounded from the dark wheel-chamber where the water was rushing under the wheel and jarring it with its tumult. At eight o'clock the woodshed was flooded and water began to creep under the kitchen door. Dorothy and the boys carried armfuls of wood and stacked them in the passage to the sitting-room, two steps higher up. At nine o'clock the boys were sent protesting to bed, and Dorothy, looking out of their window as she fumbled about in the dark for a pair of Shep's trousers that needed mending, saw a lantern flickering up the road. It was Evesham on his way to the mill-dams. The light glimmered on his oilskin coat as he climbed the stile behind the well-curb.

"He raised the flood-gates at noon," Dorothy said to herself. "I wonder if he is anxious about the dams." She resolved to watch for his return, but she was busy settling her mother for the night when she heard his footsteps on the porch. The roar of water from the hills startled Dorothy as she opened the door; it had increased in violence within an hour. A gust of wind and rain followed Evesham into the entry.

"Come in," she said, running lightly across the sitting-room to close the door of her mother's room.

He stood opposite her on the hearth-rug and looked into her eyes, across the estrangement of the summer. It was not Dorothy of the mill-head, or of Slocum's meadow, or the cold maid of the well; it was a very anxious, lonely little girl in a crumbling old house, with a foot of water in the cellar and a sick mother in the next room. She had forgotten about Ephraim and his idols; she picked up Shep's trousers from the rug, where she had dropped them, and, looking intently at her thimble finger, told him she was very glad that he had come.

"Did you think I would not come?" said he. "I'm going to take you home with me, Dorothy—you and your mother and the boys. It's not fit for you to be here alone."

"Does thee know of any danger?"

"I know of none, but water's a thing you can't depend on. It's an ugly rain; older men than your father remember nothing like it."

"I shall be glad to have mother go, and Jimmy; the house is very damp. It's an awful night for her to be out, though."

"She *must* go!" said Evesham. "You must all go. I'll be back in half an hour—"

"*I* shall not go," Dorothy said; "the boys and I must stay and look after the stock."

"What's that?" Evesham was listening to a trickling of water outside the door.

"Oh! it's from the kitchen. The door has blown open, I guess."

Dorothy looked out into the passage; a strong wind was blowing in from the kitchen, where the water covered the floor and washed against the chimney.

"This is a nice state of things! What's all this wood here for?"

"The woodshed's under water."

"You must get yourself ready, Dorothy. I'll come for your mother first in the chaise."

"I cannot go," she said. "I don't believe there is any danger. This old house has stood for eighty years; it's not likely this is the first big rain in all that time." Dorothy's spirits had risen. "Besides, I have a family of orphans to take care of. See here," she said, stooping over a basket in the shadow of the chimney. It was the "hospital tent," and as she uncovered it, a brood of belated chickens stretched out their thin necks with plaintive peeps.

Dorothy covered them with her hands and they nestled with comfortable twitterings into silence.

"You're a kind of special providence, aren't you, Dorothy? But I've no sympathy with chickens who will be born just in time for the equinoctial."

"*I* didn't want them," said Dorothy, anxious to defend her management. "The old hen stole her nest and she left them the day before the rain. She's making herself comfortable now in the corn-bin."

"She ought to be made an example of; that's the way of the world, however—retribution doesn't fall always on the right shoulders. I must go now. We'll take your mother and Jimmy first, and then, if you *won't* come, you shall let me stay with you. The mill is safe enough, anyhow."

Evesham returned with the chaise and a man, who, he insisted, should drive away old John and the cows, so that Dorothy should have less care. The mother was packed into the chaise with a vast collection of wraps, which almost obliterated Jimmy. As they started, Dorothy ran out in the rain with her mother's spectacles and the five letters, which always lay in a box on the table by her bed. Evesham took her gently by the arms and lifted her back across the puddles to the stoop.

As the chaise drove off, she went back into the sitting-room and crouched on the rug, her wet hair shining in the firelight. She took out her chickens one by one and held them under her chin, with tender words and finger-touches. If September chickens have feelings as susceptible as their bodies, Dorothy's orphans must have been imperiled by her caresses.

"Look here, Dorothy! Where's my trousers?" cried Shep, opening the door at the foot of the stairs.

Reuby was behind him, fully arrayed in his own garment aforesaid, and carrying the bedroom candle.

"Here they are—with a needle in them," said Dorothy. "What are you getting up in the middle of the night for?"

"Well, I guess it's time somebody's up. Who's that man driving off our cows?"

"Goosey! It's Walter Evesham's man. He came for mother and all of us, and he's taken old John and the cows to save us so much foddering."

"Ain't we going too?"

"I don't see why we should, just because there happens to be a little water in the kitchen. I've often seen it come in there before."

"Well, thee never saw anything like *this* before—nor anybody else, either," said Shep.

"I don't care," said Reuby, "I wish there'd come a reg'lar flood. We could climb up in the mill-loft and go sailin' down over Jordan's meadows. Wouldn't Luke Jordan open that big mouth of his to see us heave in sight about cock-crow, wing and wing, and the old tackle a-swingin'!"

"Do hush!" said Dorothy. "We may have to try it yet."

"There's an awful roarin' from our window," said Shep. "Thee can't half hear it down here. Come out on the stoop. The old ponds have got their dander up this time."

They opened the door and listened, standing together on the low step. There was, indeed, a hoarse murmur from the hills, which grew louder as they listened.

"Now she's comin'! There goes the stable-door. There was only one hinge left, anyway," said Reuby. "Mighty! Look at that wave!"

It crashed through the gate, swept across the garden and broke at their feet, sending a thin sheet of water over the floor of the porch.

"Now it's gone into the entry. Why didn't thee shut the door, Shep?"

"Well, I think we'd better clear out, anyhow. Let's go over to the mill. Say, Dorothy, shan't we?"

"Wait. There comes another wave."

The second onset was not so violent; but they hastened to gather together a few blankets, and the boys filled their pockets with cookies, with a delightful sense of unusualness and peril almost equal to a shipwreck or an attack by Indians. Dorothy took her unlucky chickens under her cloak, and they made a rush all together across the road and up the slope to the mill.

"Why didn't we think to bring a lantern?" said Dorothy, as they huddled together on the platform of the scale. "Will thee go back after one, Shep?"

"If Reuby'll go, too."

"Well, *my* legs are wet enough now. What's the use of a lantern? Mighty Moses! What's that?"

"The old mill's got under way," cried Shep. "*She's* going to tune up for Kingdom Come."

A furious head of water was rushing along the race; the great wheel creaked and swung over, and with a shudder the old mill awoke from its long sleep. The cogs clenched their teeth, the shafting shook and rattled, the stones whirled merrily round.

"Now she goes it!" cried Shep, as the humming increased to a tremor, and the tremor to a wild, unsteady din, till the timbers shook and the bolts and windows rattled. "I just wish father could hear them old stones hum."

"Oh, this is awful!" said Dorothy. She was shivering and sick with terror at this unseemly midnight revelry of her grandfather's old mill. It was as if it had awakened in a fit of delirium, and given itself up to a wild travesty of its years of peaceful work.

Shep was creeping about in the darkness.

"Look here! We've got to stop this clatter somehow. The stones are hot now. The whole thing'll burn up like tinder if we can't chock her wheels."

"Shep! Does thee *mean* it?"

"Thee'll see if I don't. Thee won't need any lantern either."

"Can't we break away the race?"

"Oh, there's a way to stop it. There's the tip-trough, but it's downstairs and we can't reach the pole."

"I'll go," said Dorothy.

"It's outside, thee knows. Thee'll get awful wet, Dorothy."

"Well, I'd just as soon be drowned as burned up. Come with me to the head of the stairs."

They felt their way hand in hand in the darkness, and Dorothy went down alone. She had forgotten about the "tip-trough," but she understood its significance. In a few moments a cascade shot out over the wheel, sending the water far into the garden.

"Right over my chrysanthemum bed," sighed Dorothy.

The wheel swung slower and slower, the mocking tumult subsided, and the old mill sank into sleep again.

There was nothing now to drown the roaring of the floods and the steady drive of the storm.

"There's a lantern," Shep called from the door. He had opened the upper half and was shielding himself behind it. "I guess it's Evesham coming back for us. He's a pretty good sort of a fellow after all; don't thee think so, Dorothy? He owes us something for drowning us out at the sheep-washing."

"What does all this mean?" said Dorothy, as Evesham swung himself over the half-door and his lantern showed them to each other in their various phases of wetness.

"There's a big leak in the lower dam; I've been afraid of it all along; there's something wrong in the principle of the thing."

Dorothy felt as if he had called her grandfather a fraud, and her father a delusion and a snare. She had grown up in the belief that the mill-dams were part of Nature's original plan in laying the foundations of the hills; but it was no time to be resentful, and the facts were against her.

"Dorothy," said Evesham, as he tucked the buffalo about her, "this is the second time I've tried to save you from drowning, but you never will wait. I'm all ready to be a hero, but you won't be a heroine."

"I'm too practical for a heroine," said Dorothy. "There! I've forgotten my chickens."

"I'm glad of it. Those chickens were a mistake. They oughtn't to be perpetuated."

Youth and happiness can stand a great deal of cold water; but it was not to be expected that Rachel Barton would be especially benefited by her night journey through the floods. Evesham waited in the hall when he heard the door of her room open next morning. Dorothy came slowly down the stairs; he knew by her lingering-step and the softly closed door that she was not happy.

"Mother is very sick," she answered his inquiry. "It is like the turn of inflammation and rheumatism she had once before. It will be very slow— and oh, it is such suffering! Why do the best women in the world have to suffer so?"

"Will you let me talk things over with you after breakfast, Dorothy?"

"Oh yes," she said, "there is so much to do and think about. I wish father would come home!"

The tears came into Dorothy's eyes as she looked at him. Rest, such as she had never known or felt the need of till now, and strength immeasurable, since it would multiply her own by an unknown quantity, stood within reach of her hand, but she might not put it out.

Evesham was dizzy with the struggle between longing and resolution. He had braced his nerves for a long and hungry waiting, but fate had yielded suddenly; the floods had brought her to him—his flotsam and jetsam more precious than all the guarded treasures of the earth. She had come, with all her girlish, unconscious beguilements, and all her womanly cares and anxieties too. He must strive against her sweetness, while he helped her to bear her burdens.

"Now about the boys, Dorothy," he said, two hours later, as they stood together by the fire in the low, oak-finished room, which was his office and book-room. The door was ajar so that Dorothy might hear her mother's bell. "Don't you think they had better be sent to school somewhere?"

"Yes," said Dorothy, "they ought to go to school—but—well, I may as well tell thee the truth. There's very little to do it with. We've had a poor summer. I suppose I've managed badly, and mother has been sick a good while."

"You've forgotten about the pond-rent, Dorothy."

"No," she said, with a quick flush, "I hadn't forgotten it, but I couldn't *ask* thee for it."

"I spoke to your father about monthly payments, but he said better leave it to accumulate for emergencies. Shouldn't you call this an 'emergency,' Dorothy?"

"But does thee think we ought to ask rent for a pond that has all leaked away?"

"Oh, there's pond enough left, and I've used it a dozen times over this summer. I should be ashamed to tell you, Dorothy, how my horn has been exalted in your father's absence. However, retribution has overtaken me at last; I'm responsible, you know, for all the damage last night. It was in the agreement that I should keep up the dams."

"Oh!" said Dorothy; "is thee sure?"

Evesham laughed.

"If your father was like any other man, Dorothy, he'd make me 'sure,' when he gets home. I will defend myself to this extent; I've patched and propped them all summer, after every rain, and tried to provide for the fall storms; but there's a flaw in the original plan—"

"Thee said that once before," said Dorothy. "I wish thee wouldn't say it again."

"Why not?"

"Because I love those old mill-dams. I've trotted over them ever since I could walk alone."

"You shall trot over them still. We will make them as strong as the everlasting hills. They shall outlast our time, Dorothy."

"Well, about the rent," said Dorothy. "I'm afraid it will not take us through the winter, unless there is something I can do. Mother couldn't possibly be moved now; and if she could, it will be months before the house is fit to live in. But we cannot stay here in comfort, unless thy mother will let me make up in some way. Mother will not need me all the time, and I know thy mother hires women to spin."

"She'll let you do all you like if it will make you any happier. But you don't know how much money is coming to you. Come, let us look over the figures."

He lowered the lid of the black mahogany secretary, placed a chair for Dorothy and opened a great ledger before her, bending down, with one hand on the back of the chair, the other turning the leaves of the ledger. Considering the index and the position of the letter B in the alphabet, he was a long time finding his place. Dorothy looked out of the window over the tops of the yellowing woods to the gray and turbid river below. Where the hemlocks darkened the channel of the glen she heard the angry floods rushing down. The formless rain mists hung low and hid the opposite shore.

"See!" said Evesham, his finger wandering rather vaguely down the page. "Your father went away on the 3d of May. The first month's rent came due on the 3d of June. That was the day I opened the gate and let the water down on you, Dorothy. I'm responsible for everything, you see—even for the old ewe that was drowned."

His words came in a dream as he bent over her, resting his unsteady hand heavily on the ledger.

Dorothy laid her cheek on the date that she could not see and burst into tears.

"Don't—please don't!" he said, straightening himself and locking his hands behind him. "I am human, Dorothy."

The weeks of Rachel's sickness that followed were perhaps the best discipline Evesham's life had ever known. He held the perfect flower of his bliss unclosing in his hand; yet he might barely permit himself to breathe its fragrance. His mother had been a strong and prosperous woman; there had been little he had ever been able to do for her. It was well for him to feel the weight of helpless infirmity in his arms as he lifted Dorothy's mother from side to side of her bed, while Dorothy's hands smoothed the coverings. It was well for him to see the patient endurance of suffering, such as his youth and strength defied. It was bliss to wait on Dorothy and follow her with little watchful homages, received with a shy wonder which was delicious to him; for Dorothy's nineteen years had been too full of service to others to leave much room for dreams of a kingdom of her own. Her silent presence in her mother's sick-room awed him. Her gentle, decisive voice and ways, her composure and unshaken endurance through nights of watching and days of anxious confinement and toil, gave him a new reverence for the powers and mysteries of her unfathomable woman-hood.

The time of Friend Barton's return drew near. It must be confessed that Dorothy welcomed it with something of dread, and that Evesham did not welcome it at all. On the contrary, the thought of it roused all his latent obstinacy and aggressiveness. The first day or two after the momentous arrival wore a good deal upon every member of the family, except Margaret Evesham, who was provided with a philosophy of her own, that amounted almost to a gentle obtuseness and made her a comfortable non-conductor, preventing more electric souls from shocking each other.

On the morning of the fourth day, Dorothy came out of her mother's room with a tray of empty dishes in her hands. She saw Evesham at the stair-head and hovered about in the shadowy part of the hall till he should go down.

"Dorothy," he said, "I'm waiting for you." He took the tray from her and rested it on the banisters. "Your father and I have talked over all the business. He's got the impression that I'm one of the most generous fellows in the world. I intend to leave him in that delusion for the present. Now may I speak to him about something else, Dorothy? Have I not waited long enough for my heart's desire?"

"Take care," said Dorothy softly—"thee'll upset the tea-cups."

"Confound the tea-cups!" He stooped to place the irrelevant tray on the floor, but now Dorothy was halfway down the staircase. He caught her on the landing, and taking both her hands drew her down on the step beside him.

"Dorothy, this is the second time you've taken advantage of my trusting nature. This time you shall be punished. You needn't try to hide your face, you little traitor. There's no repentance in you!"

"If I'm to be punished there's no need of repentance."

"Oh, is that your Quaker doctrine? Dorothy, do you know, I've never heard you speak my name, except once, and then you were angry with me."

"When was that?"

"The night I caught you at the gate. You said, 'I had rather have one of those dumb brutes for company than thee, Walter Evesham.' You said it in the fiercest little voice. Even the 'thee' sounded as if you hated me."

"I did," said Dorothy promptly. "I had reason to."

"Do you hate me now, Dorothy?"

"Not so much as I did then."

"What an implacable little Quaker you are."

"A tyrant is always hated," said Dorothy, trying to release her hands.

"If you will look in my eyes, Dorothy, and call me by my name, just once, I'll let 'thee' go."

"Walter Evesham," said Dorothy, with great firmness and decision.

"No, that won't do! You must look at me, and say it softly, in a little sentence, Dorothy."

"Will thee please let me go, Walter?"

Walter Evesham was a man of his word, but as Dorothy sped away, he looked as if he wished that he was not.

The next evening Friend Barton sat by his wife's easy-chair drawn into the circle of firelight, with his elbows on his knees and his head between his hands.

The worn spot on the top of his head had widened considerably during the summer, but Rachel looked stronger and brighter than she had done for many a day. There was even a little flush on her cheek, but this might have come from the excitement of a long talk with her husband.

"I'm sorry thee takes it so hard, Thomas. I was afraid thee would. But the way didn't seem to open for me to do much. I can see now that Dorothy's inclinations have been turning this way for some time; though it's not likely she would own it, poor child; and Walter Evesham's not one who is easily gainsaid. If thee could only feel differently about it, I can't say but that it would make me very happy to see Dorothy's heart satisfied. Can't thee bring thyself into unity with it, father? He's a nice young man. They're nice folks. Thee can't complain of the blood. Margaret Evesham tells me a cousin of hers married one of the Lawrences, so we are kind of kin after all."

"I don't complain of the blood; they're well enough placed, as far as the world is concerned. But their ways are not our ways, Rachel; their faith is not our faith."

"Well, I can't see such a very great difference, come to live among them. 'By their fruits ye shall know them.' To comfort the widow and the fatherless, and keep ourselves unspotted from the world;—thee's always preached that, father. I really can't see any more worldliness here than among many households with us; and I'm sure if we haven't been the widow and the fatherless this summer, we've been next to it."

Friend Barton raised his head: "Rachel," he said, "look at that!" He pointed upward to an ancient sword with belt and trappings which gleamed on the paneled chimney-piece, crossed by an old queen's-arm. Evesham had given up his large, sunny room to Dorothy's mother, but he had not removed all his lares and penates.

"Yes, dear; that's his grandfather's sword—Colonel Evesham, who was killed at Saratoga."

"Why does he hang up that thing of abomination for a light and a guide to his footsteps, if his way be not far from ours?"

"Why, father! Colonel Evesham was a good man. I dare say he fought for the same reason that thee preaches, because he felt it to be his duty."

"I find no fault with him, Rachel. Doubtless he followed his light, as thee says, but he followed it in better ways too. He cleared land and built a homestead and a meeting-house. Why doesn't his grandson hang up his old broadaxe and plowshare and worship them, if he must have idols, instead of that symbol of strife and bloodshed. Does thee want our Dorothy's children to grow up under the shadow of the sword?"

There was a stern light of prophecy in the old man's eyes.

"May be Walter Evesham would take it down," said Rachel simply, leaning back and closing her eyes. "I never was much of a hand to argue, even if I had the strength for it; but it would hurt me a good deal—I must say it—if thee should deny Dorothy in this matter, Thomas. It's a very serious thing for old folks to try to turn young hearts the way they think they ought to go. I remember now—I was thinking about it last night, and it all came back as fresh—I don't know that I ever told thee about that young Friend who visited me before I heard thee preach at Stony Valley? Well, father, he was wonderful pleased with him, but I didn't feel any drawing that way. He urged me a good deal, more than was pleasant for either of us. He wasn't at all reconciled to thee, Thomas, if thee remembers."

"I remember," said Thomas Barton. "It was an anxious time."

"Well, dear, if father *had* insisted and had sent thee away, I can't say but life would have been a very different thing to me."

"I thank thee for saying it, Rachel." Friend Barton's head drooped. "Thee has suffered much through me; thee's had a hard life, but thee's been well beloved."

The flames leaped and flickered in the chimney; they touched the wrinkled hands whose only beauty was in their deeds; they crossed the room and lit the pillows where, for three generations, young heads had dreamed and gray heads had watched and wearied; then they mounted to the chimney and struck a gleam from the sword.

"Well, father," said Rachel, "what answer is thee going to give Walter Evesham?"

"I shall say no more, my dear. Let the young folks have their way.

There's strife and contention enough in the world without my stirring up more. And it may be I'm resisting the Master's will. I left her in his care; this may be his way of dealing with her."

Walter Evesham did not take down his grandfather's sword. Fifty years later another went up beside it, the sword of a young Evesham who never left the field of Shiloh; and beneath them both hangs the portrait of the Quaker grandmother, Dorothy Evesham, at the age of sixty-nine.

The golden ripples, silver now, are hidden under a "round-eared cap;" the quick flush has faded in her cheek, and fold upon fold of snowy gauze and creamy silk are crossed over the bosom that once thrilled to the fiddles of Slocum's barn. She has found the cool grays and the still waters; but on Dorothy's children rests the "Shadow of the Sword."

THE STORY OF THE ALCAZAR

It was told by Captain John to a boy from the mainland who was spending the summer on the Island, as they sat together one August evening at sunset, on a broken bowsprit which had once been a part of the Alcazar.

It was dead low water in Southwest Harbor, a land-locked inlet that nearly cut the Island in two, and was the gateway through which the fishing-craft from the village at the harbor head found their way out into the great Penobscot Bay. There were many days during the stern winter and bleak spring months when the gate was blocked with ice or veiled in fog, but nature relented a little toward the Island folk in the fall and sent them sunny days for their late, scant harvesting, and steady winds for the mackerel-fishing, to give them a little hope before the winter set in sharp with the equinoctial. Now, at low tide, the bright gateway shone wide open, as if to let out the waters that rise and fall ten feet in the inlet. You could look far out, beyond the lighthouse on Creenlaw's Neck and the islands that throng the mouth of the harbor, to the red spot of flame the sunset had kindled below the rack of smoke-gray clouds. The color burned in a dull gleam upon the water, broken by the dark shapes of shadowy islands; the sail-boats at anchor in the muddy, glistening flats leaned over disconsolately on their sides, in despair of ever again feeling the thrill of the returning waters beneath their keels; and the gray, weather-beaten houses crowded together on the brink of the cliff above the beach, looking like a group of hooded old women watching for a belated sail, seemed to have caught the expression of their inmates' lives. At high tide the hulk of the Alcazar had been full of water, which was now pouring out through a hole in the planking of her side in a continuous, murmurous stream, like the voice of a persistent talker in a silent company. The old ship looked much too big for her narrow grave at the foot of the green cliff, in which her anchor was deeply sunk and half overgrown with thistles. Her blunt bow and the ragged stump of the figure-head rose, dark and high, above the wet beach where Captain John sat with his absorbed listener. There were rifts about her rail where the red sunset looked through. Her naked sides, that for years had been moistened only by the perennial rains and snows, showed rough and scaly like the armor of some fabled sea-monster. She was tethered to the cliff by her rusty anchor-chain that swung across the space between, serving as a clothes-line for the draggled driftweed left by the receding tide to dry.

"She was a big ship for these parts," Captain John was saying. "There wan't one like her ever come into these waters before. Lord! folks come down from the Neck, and from Green's Landin', and Nor'east Harbor, and I don't know but they come from the main, to see her when she was fust towed in. And such work as they made of her name! Some called it one way and some another. It's a kind of a Cubian name, they say. I expect there ain't anybody round here that can call it right. However 'twas, old Cap'n Green took and pried it off her starboard quarter, and somebody got hold of it and nailed it up over the blacksmith's shop; and there you can see it now. The old cap'n named her the Stranger when he had her refitted. May be you could make out the tail of an S on her stern if you could git around there. That name's been gone these forty year; seem's if she never owned to it, and it didn't stick to her. She was never called anythin' but the Alcazar, long as ever I knew her, and I expect I know full's much about her as anybody round here. 'Twas a-settin' here on this very beach at low water, just's we be now, that the old man told me fust how he picked her up. It took a wonderful holt on him, there's no doubt about that. He told it to me more 'n once before the time come when he was to put the finish on to it; but in a gen'ral way the cap'n wan't much of a talker, and he was shy of this partic'lar business, for reasons that I expect nobody knows much about. But a man most always likes to talk to somebody, no matter how close-mouthed he may be. 'Twas just about this time o' year, fall of '27, the year Parson Flavor was ordained, Cap'n Green had gone a-mack'rel-fishin' with his two boys off Isle au Haut, and they did think o' cruisin' out into Frenchman's Bay if the weather hel' steady. They was havin' fair luck, hangin' round the island off and on for a matter of a week, when it thickened up a little and set in foggy, and for two days they didn't see the shore. The second evenin' the wind freshened from the south'ard and east'ard and drove the fog in shore a bit, and the sun, just before he set, looked like a big yellow ball through the fog and made a sickly kind of a glimmer over the water. They was a-lyin' at anchor, and all of a sudden, right to the wind'ard of 'em, this old ship loomed up, driftin' in with the wind and flood-tide. They couldn't make her out, and I guess for a minute the old cap'n didn't know but it was the Flyin' Dutchman; but she hadn't a rag o' sail on her, and as she got nearer they could see there wan't a man on board. The cap'n didn't like the looks of her, but he knew she wan't no phantom, and he and one of his boys down with the punt and went alongside. 'Twan't more 'n a quarter of a mile to her. They hailed and couldn't git no answer. They knew she was a furriner by her build, and she must 'a' been a long time at sea by her havin' barnacles on her nigh as big's a mack'rel kit. Finally, they pulled up to her fore—chains and clum aboard of her. I never see a ship abandoned at sea, myself, but I ain't no doubt but what it made 'em feel kind o' shivery when they looked aft along her decks, and not a soul in sight, and every-thin' bleached, and gray, and iron-rusted, and the riggin' all slack and white's though it had been chawed, and nothin' left of her sails but some old rags flappin' like a last year's scarecrow. They went and looked in the fo'k'sel: there wan't nothin' there but some chists, men's chists, with a little old beddin' left in the bunks. They went down the companion-way: cabin-door unlocked, everything in there as nat'ral's though it had just been left, only 'twas kind o' mouldy-smellin'. I expect the cap'n give a kind of a start as he looked around. 'Twan't no old greasy whaler's cabin, nor no packet-ship neither. There wan't many craft like her on the seas in them days. She was fixed up inside more like a gentleman's yacht is now. Merchantmen in them days didn't have their Turkey carpets and their colored wine-glasses jinglin' in the racks. While they was explorin' round in there, movin' round kind o' cautious, the door of the cap'n's stateroom swung open with a creak, just's though somebody was a-shovin' it slow like, and the ship give a kind of a stir and a rustlin', moanin' sound, as if she was a-comin' to life. The old man never made no secret but what he was scairt when he went through her that night. 'Twan't so much what he said as the way he looked when he told it. I expect he thought he'd seen enough, about the time that door blew open. He said he knowed 'twas nothin' but a puff o' wind struck her, and that he'd better be a-gittin' on to his own craft before he lost her in the fog. So he went back and got under weigh, and sent a line aboard of the stranger and took her in tow, and all that night with a good southeast wind they kept a-movin' toward home. The old man was kind o' res'less and wakeful, walkin' the decks and lookin' over the stern at the big ship follerin' him like a ghost. The moonlight was a little dull with fog, but he could see her, plain, a-comin' on before the wind with her white riggin' and bare poles, and hear the water sousin' under her bows. He said 'twas in his mind more 'n a dozen times to cut her adrift. You see he had his misgivin's about her from the fust, though he never let on what they was; but he hung on to her as a man will, sometimes, agin feelin's that have more sense in 'em than reason, like as not. He knew everybody at the Harbor would laugh at him for lettin' go such a prize as that just for a notion, and it wan't his way, you may be sure; he didn't need no one to tell him what she was wuth. Anyhow he hung to her, and next day they beached her at high water, right over there by the old ship-yard. He took Deacon S'lvine and his brother-in-law, Cap'n Purse—Pierce they call it nowadays, but in the cap'n's time 'twas Purse. That sounds kind o' broad and comfortable, like the cap'n's wescoat; but the family's thinnin' down a good deal lately and gettin' kind o' sharp and lean, and may be Pierce is more suitable. But 's I was sayin', Cap'n Green took them two—cheerful, loud-talkin' men they was both of 'em—aboard of her to go through her, for he hadn't no notion o' goin' into that cap'n's stateroom alone, even in broad daylight; but 'twan't there the secret of her lay; there wan't nothin' in there to scare anybody. She was trimmed up, I tell you, just elegant. Real mahogany, none of your veneerin', but the real stuff; lace curt'ins to the berth, lace on the pillows, and a satin coverlid, rumpled up as though the cap'n had just turned out; and there was his slippers handy—the greatest-lookin' slippers for a man you ever saw. They wouldn't 'a' been too big for the neatest-footed woman in the Harbor. But Land! they was just thick with mould, and so was everythin' in the place, even to an old gittar with the strings most rotted off of it, and the picters of furrin-lookin' women on the walls—trinin'-lookin' creeturs most of 'em. They hunted all through his desk, but couldn't find no log. 'Twas plain enough that whoever'd left that ship had took pains that she shouldn't tell no tales, and 'twan't long before they found out the reason.

"When they come to go below—there was considerable of a crowd on deck by that time, standin' round while they knocked out the keys and took off the fore-hatch—Cap'n Green called on Cap'n Purse and the deacon to go down with him; but they didn't 'pear to be very anxious, and the old man wan't goin' to hang back for company with everybody lookin' at him, so he lit a candle and went down, and the folks crowded round and waited for him. I was there myself, 's close to him as I be to that fish barrel, when he come up, his face white 's a sheet and the candle shakin' in his hand, and sot down on the hatch-combin'.

" 'Give me room!' says he, kind o' leanin' back on the crowd. 'Give me air, can't you? She's full o' dead niggers. She's a slaver.'

"Now, 'twas the talk pretty gen'rally that the cap'n had had a hand in that business himself in his early days, and that it set uncomfortable on him afterwards. It never was known how he'd got his money. He didn't have any to begin with. He was always a kind of a lone bird and dug his way along up somehow. Nobody knows what was workin' on him while he sot there; he looked awful sick. It was kind of quiet for a minute, but them that couldn't see him kep' pushin' for'ards and callin' out: 'What d'you see? What's down there?' And them close by wanted to know, all talkin' to once, why he thought she was a slaver, and how long the niggers had been dead. Lord! what a fuss there was. Everybody askin' the foolishest questions, and crowdin' and squeezin', and them in front pushin' back away from the hatchway, as if they expected the dead would rise and walk out o' that black hole where they'd laid so long. They couldn't get much out o' the old man, except that there was skel'tons scattered all over the after hold, and that he knew she was a slaver by the way she was fixed up. '*How*'d he know?' folks asked amongst themselves; but nobody liked to ask the cap'n. As for how long them Africans had been dead, they had to find that out for themselves—all they ever did find out—for the cap'n wouldn't talk about it, and he wouldn't go down in her again. It 'peared's if he was satisfied.

"Wal, it made a terrible stir in the place. As I tell you, they come from fifty mile around to see her. They had it all in the papers. Some had one idee and some another about the way she come to be abandoned, all in good shape and them human bein's in her hold. Some said ship-fever, some said mutiny; but when they come to look her over and found there wan't a water-cask aboard of her that hadn't s'runk up and gone to pieces, they settled down on the notion that she was a Spanish or a Cubian slaver, or may be a Portagee, got short o' water in the horse-latitudes; cap'n and crew left her in the boats, and the niggers—Lord! it makes a body sick to think o' them. That was always my the'ry 'bout her—short o' water; but some folks wan't satisfied 'thout somethin' more ex-citin'. 'Twan't enough for 'em to have all them creeturs dyin' down there by inches. They stuck to it about some blood-stains on the linin' in her hold, but I tell you the difference between old blood-stains and rust that's may be ten or fifteen years old's might' hard to tell.

"Nobody knows what the old cap'n was thinkin' about in them days. 'Twas full three month or more 'fore he went aboard of her ag'in. He let it be known about that he wanted to sell her, but he couldn't git an offer even; nobody seemed to want to take hold of her. Winter set in early and the ice blocked her in, and there she lay, the lonesomest thing in sight. You never see no child'n climbin' 'round on her, and there was a story that queer noises like moanin' and clankin' of chains come out of her on windy nights; but it might 'a' been the ice, crowdin' as she careened over and back with the risin' and fallin' tide. But when spring opened, folks used to see the old cap'n hangin' round the ship-yard and lookin' her over at low tide, where the ice had cut the barnacles off of her.

"One night in the store he figgered up how much lumber she'd carry from Bangor, and 'twan't long 'fore he had a gang o' men at work on her. It seemed's though he was kind of infatuated with her. He was 'fraid of her, but he couldn't let her alone. And she was a mighty well-built craft. Floridy pine and live-oak and mahogany from the Mosquito coast; built in Cadiz, most likely. Look at her now—she don't look to home here, does she? She never did. She's as much like our harbor craft as one o' them big, yellow-eyed, bare-necked buzzards is to one o' these here little sand-peeps. But she was a handsome vessel. Them live-oak ribs'll outlast your time, if you was to live to be old."

The two faces looked up at the hulk of the Alcazar—the blanched, wave-worn messenger sent by the tropic seas into the far North with a tale that the living had never dared to tell, and that had perished on the lips of the dead. Its shadow, spreading broad upon the beach, made the gathering twilight deeper. Out on the harbor the pale saffron light lingered, long after the red had faded. How many tides had ebbed and flowed since the old ship, chained at the foot of the cliff, had warmed in the waters of the Gulf her bare, corrugated sides, warped by the frosts, stabbed by the ice of pitiless Northern winters! Where were the sallow, dark-bearded faces that had watched from her high poop the brief twilights die on that "unshadowed main," which a century ago was the scene of some of the wildest romances and blackest crimes in maritime history—the bright, restless bosom that warmed into life a thousand serpents whose trail could be traced through the hot, flower-scented Southern plazas and courts into the peaceful white villages of the North!

"Sho! I'd no idee 'twas a-gittin' on so late," said Captain John. "There ain't anybody watchin' out for me. I kin put my family under my hat, but I don' know what your folks'll think's come o' you.

"Wal, the rest on 'twon't take long to tell. The old man had her fitted up in good shape by the time the ice was out of the river, and run her up to Bangor in ballast, and loaded her there for New York. He had an ugly trip down the coast: lost his deck load and three men overboard in a southeaster off Nantucket Shoals. It made the whole ship's company feel pretty solemn, but the old man took it the hardest of any of 'em, and from that time seems as if he lost his grip; the old scare settled back on him blacker 'n ever. There wan't a man aboard of her that liked her. They all knew her story, that she was the Alcazar from nobody knows where, instead of the Stranger from Newburyport. The cap'n had Newburyport put on to her because he was a Newburyport man and all his vessels was built there. But she hadn't more 'n touched the dock in New York before every one on 'em left her, even to the cook. 'I'm leery o' this 'ere ship,' says one big

Cornishman. 'No better than a floatin' coffin, anyway,' was what they all said of her; and I guess the cap'n would 'a' left her right there himself if it hadn't been for the money he'd put into her. I expect he was a little too fond of money, may be; but I've knowed others just as sharp's the old cap'n that didn't seem to have his luck. The mate saw him two or three times while he was a-lyin' in New York, and noticed he was drinkin' more 'n usual. He come home light and anchored off the bar, just as a southeaster was a-comin' on. It wouldn't 'a' been no trouble for him to have laid there, if he'd had good ground-gear; but there 'twas ag'in, he'd been a leetle too savin'. He'd used the old cables he found in her. The new mate didn't know nothin' about her, and he put out one anchor. The cap'n had taken a kag o' New England rum aboard and been drawin' on it pretty reg'lar all the way up, and as the gale come on he got kind o' wild and went at it harder 'n ever. About midnight the cable parted. They let go the other anchor, but it didn't snub her for a minute, and she swung, broadside to, on to the bar. The men clum into the riggin' before she struck, but the old cap'n was staggerin' 'round decks, kind o' dazed and dumb-like, not tryin' to do anythin' to save himself. The mate tried to git him into the riggin', seein' he wan't in no condition to look out for himself; but the old man struck loose from his holt and cried out to him through the noise:—

"'Let me alone! I've got to go with her. I tell ye I've got to go with her!'

"The mate just had time to swing himself back into the mizzen-shrouds before the sea broke over her and left the decks bare. The old ship pounded over the bar in an hour or so, and drifted up here on to the beach where she is now. Every man on board was saved except the cap'n. He 'went with her,' sure enough.

"There was talk enough about that thing before they got done with it to 'a' made the old man roll in his grave. They raked up all the stories about his cruisin' on the Spanish main when he was a young man. They wan't stories *he'd* ever told; he wan't much of a hand to talk about what he'd seen and done on his v'yages. They never let him rest till 'twas pretty much the gen'ral belief, and is to this day, that he knew more about that slaver from the first than he ever owned to.

"I never had much to say about it, but 'twas plain enough to me. I had my suspicions the mornin' he towed her in. He looked terrible shattered. It 'peared to me he wan't ever the same man afterwards.

"'I've got to go with her!' Them was his last words. He knew that ship and him belonged together, same as a man and his sins. He knew she'd been a-huntin' him up and down the western ocean for twenty year, with them dead o' his'n in her hold—and she'd hunted him down at last."

Captain John paused with this peroration: he dug a hole in the wet sand with the toe of his boot, and watched it slowly fill.

"'Twas a bait most any one would 'a' smelt of, a six-hundred-ton ship and every timber in her sound; but you'd 'a' thought he'd been more cautious, knowin' what he did of her. She was bound to have him, though."

"Captain John," said the boy, a little hoarse from his long silence, "what do you suppose it *was* he did? Anything except just leave them—the negroes, I mean?"

"Lord! Wan't that *enough*? To steal 'em, and then leave 'em there—battened down like rats in the hold! However, I expect there ain't anybody that can tell you the whole of that story. It's one of them mysteries that rests with the dead.

"The new mate—the young fellow he brought on from New York—he married the cap'n's daughter. None o' the Harbor boys ever seemed to jibe in with her. I always had a notion that she was a touch above most of 'em, but she and her mother was as good as a providence to them shipwrecked men when they was throwed ashore, strangers in the place and no money; and it ended in Rachel's takin' up with the mate and the whole family's leavin' the place. It was long after all the talk died away that the widow come back and lived here in the same quiet way she always had, till she was laid alongside the old cap'n. There wan't a better woman ever walked this earth than Mary Green, that was Mary Spofford."

Captain John rose from the bowsprit and rubbed his cramped knees before climbing the hill. He parted with his young listener at the top and took a lonely path across the shore-pasture to a little cabin, where no light shone, built like the nest of a sea-bird on the edge of high-water mark.

On the gray beach below, a small, dingy yawl, with one sail loosely bundled over the thwarts, leaned toward the door-latch as if listening for its click. It had an almost human expression of patient though wistful waiting. It was the poorest boat in the Harbor; it had no name painted on its stern, but Captain John, in the solitude of his watery wanderings among the islands and channels of the bay, always called her the Mary Spofford. The boy from the main went home slowly along the village street toward the many-windowed house in which his mother and sisters were boarding. There were voices, calling and singing abroad on the night air, reflected from the motionless, glimmering sheet of dark water below as from a sounding-board. Cow-bells tinkled away among the winding paths along the low, dim shores. The night-call of the heron from the muddy flats struck sharply across the stillness, and from the outer bay came the murmur of the old ground-swell, which never rests, even in the calmest weather.

A CLOUD ON THE MOUNTAIN

Ruth Mary stood on the high river bank, looking along the beach below to see if her small brother Tommy was lurking anywhere under the willows with his fishing-pole. He had been sent half an hour before to the earth cellar for potatoes, and Ruth Mary's father, Mr. Tully, was waiting for his dinner.

She did not see Tommy; but while she lingered, looking at the river hurrying down the shoot between the hills and curling up over the pebbles of the bar, she saw a team of bay horses and a red-wheeled wagon come rattling down the stony slope of the opposite shore. In the wagon she counted four men. Three of them wore white, helmet-shaped hats that made brilliant spots of light against the bank. The horses were driven half their length into the stream and allowed to drink, as well as they could for the swiftness of the current, while the men seemed to consult together, the two on the front seat turning back to speak with the two behind, and pointing across the river.

Ruth Mary watched them with much interest, for travelers such as these seemed to be seldom came as far up Bear River valley as the Tullys' cattle range. The visitors who came to them were mostly cow-boys looking up stray cattle, or miners on their way to the "Banner district," or packers with mule trains going over the mountains, to return in three weeks, or three months, as their journey prospered. Fishermen and hunters came up into the hills in the season of trout and deer, but they came as a rule on horseback, and at a distance were hardly to be distinguished from the cow-boys and the miners.

The men in the wagon were evidently strangers to that locality. They had seen Ruth Mary watching them from the hill, and now one of them rose up in the wagon and shouted across to her, pointing to the river.

She could not hear his words for the noise of the ripple and of the wind which blew freshly down-stream, but she understood that he was inquiring about the ford. She motioned up the river and called to him, though she knew her words could not reach him, to keep on the edge of the ripple. Her gestures, however, aided by the driver's knowledge of fords, were sufficient; he turned his horses up-stream and they took water at the place she had tried to indicate. The wagon sank to the wheel-hubs; the horses kept their feet well, though the current was strong; the sun shone brightly on the white hats and laughing faces of the men, on the guns in their hands, on the red paint of the wagon and the warm backs of the

71

horses breasting the stream. When they were halfway across, one of the men tossed a small, reluctant black dog over the wheel into the river, and all the company, with the exception of the driver, who was giving his attention to his horses, broke into hilarious shouts of encouragement to the swimmer in his struggle with the current. It was carrying him down and would have landed him, without effort of his own, on a strip of white sand beach under the willows above the bend; but now the unhappy little object, merely a black nose and two blinking anxious eyes above the water, had drifted into an eddy, from which he cast forlorn glances toward his faithless friends in the wagon. The dog was in no real peril, but Ruth Mary did not know this, and her heart swelled with indignant pity. Only shyness kept her from wading to his rescue. Now one of the laughing young men, thinking the joke had gone far enough perhaps, and reckless of a wetting, leaped out into the water, and, plunging along in his high boots, soon had the terrier by the scruff of his neck, and waded ashore with his sleek, quivering little body nestled in the bosom of his flannel hunting shirt.

A deep cut in the bank, through which the wagon was dragged, was screened by willows. When the fording party had arrived at the top, Ruth Mary was nowhere to be seen. "Where's that girl got to all of a sudden?" one of the men demanded. They had intended to ask her several questions; but she was gone, and the road before them plainly led to the low-roofed cabin, and loosely built barn with straw and daylight showing through its cracks, the newly planted poplar-trees above the thatched earth cellar, and all the signs of a tentative home in this solitude of the hills.

They drove on slowly, the young man who had waded ashore, whom his comrades addressed as Kirkwood or Kirk, walking behind the wagon with the dog in his arms, responding to his whimpering claims for attention with teasing caresses. The dog, it seemed, was the butt as well as the pet of the party. As they approached the house he scrambled out of Kirkwood's arms and lingered to take a roll in the sandy path, coming up a moment afterward to be received with blighting sarcasms upon his appearance. After his ignominious wetting he was quite unable to bear up under them, and slunk to the rear with deprecatory blinks and waggings of his tail whenever one of the men looked back.

Ruth Mary had run home quickly to tell her father, who was sitting in the sun by the wood-pile, of the arrival of strangers from across the river. Mr. Tully rose up deliberately and went to meet his guests, keeping between his teeth the sliver of pine he had been chewing while waiting for his dinner. It helped to bear him out in that appearance of indifference he thought it well to assume, as if such arrivals were an every-day occurrence.

"Hasn't Tommy got back yet, mother?" Ruth Mary asked as she entered the house. Mrs. Tully was a stout, low-browed woman, with grayish yellow hair of that dry and lifeless texture which shows declining health or want of care. Her blue eyes looked faded in the setting of her tanned complexion. She sat in a low chair, her knees wide apart, defined by her limp calico draperies, rocking a child of two years, a fat little girl with flushed cheeks and flaxen hair braided into tight knots on her forehead, who was asleep in the large cushioned rocking-chair in the middle of the room. The room was somewhat bare, for the shed-room outside was evidently the more used part of the house. The cook stove was there in the inclosed corner, and beside it a table and shelf with a tin hand-basin hanging beneath, while the crannies of the logs on each side of the doorway were utilized as shelves for all the household articles in frequent requisition that were not hanging from nails driven into the logs, or from the projecting roof-poles against the light.

Tommy had not returned, and Mrs. Tully suggested as a reason for his delay that he had stopped somewhere to catch grasshoppers for bait.

"I should think he had enough of 'em in that bottle of his," Ruth Mary said, "to last him till the 'hoppers come again. Some strange men forded the river just now. Father's gone to speak to them. I guess he'll ask 'em to stop to dinner."

Mrs. Tully got up heavily and went to the door. "Here, Angy—" she addressed a girl of eight or ten years who sat on the flat boulder that was the cabin doorstep;—"you go get them taters; that's a good girl," she added coaxingly, as Angy did not stir. "If your foot hurts you, you can walk on your heel."

Angy, who was complaining of a stone-bruise, got up and limped away, upsetting from her lap as she rose two kittens of tender years, who tumbled over each other before getting their legs under them, and staggered off, steering themselves jerkily with their tails.

"Oh, Angy!" Ruth Mary remonstrated, but she could not stay to comfort the kittens. She ran up the short, crooked stairs leading to the garret bedroom which she shared with Angy, hastily to put on her shoes and stockings and brace her pretty figure, under the blue calico waist she wore, with her first pair of stays, an important purchase made on her last visit to the town in the valley, and to be worn now, if ever. It was hot at noon in the bedroom under the roof, and by the time Ruth Mary had fortified herself to meet the eyes of strangers she was uncomfortably flushed, and short of breath besides from the pressure of the new stays. She went slowly down the uneven stairs, wishing that she could walk as softly in her shoes as she could barefoot.

Her father was talking to the strangers in the shed-room. They seemed tall and formidable, under the low roof, against the flat glare of the sun on the hard-swept ground in front of the shed. She waited inside until her mother reminded her of the dinner half cooked on the stove; then she went out shyly, the light falling on her downcast face and full white eyelids, on her yellow hair, sun-faded and meekly parted over her forehead, which was low like her mother's, but smooth as one of the white stones of the river beach. Her fair skin was burned to a clear, light red tint, and her blonde eyebrows and lashes showed silvery against it, but her chin was very white underneath, and there was a white space behind each of her little ears where her hair was knotted tightly away from her neck.

"This is my daughter," Mr. Tully said briefly; and then he gave some hospitable orders about dinner which the strangers interrupted, saying that they had brought a lunch with them and would not trouble the family until supper-time.

They gathered up their hunting gear, and lifting their hats to Ruth Mary, followed Mr. Tully, who had offered to show them the best fishing on that part of the river.

Mr. Tully explained to his wife and daughter, as the latter placed the dinner on the table, that three of the strangers were the engineers from the railroad camp at Moor's Bridge, and the fourth was a packer and teamster from the same camp; that they were all going up the river to look at timber, and wanted a little sport by the way. They had expected to keep on the other side of the river, but seeing the ranch on the opposite shore, with wheel-tracks going down to the water, they had concluded to try the ford and the fishing and ask for a night's accommodation.

"They don't want we should put ourselves out any. They're used to roughin' it, they say. If you can git together somethin' to feed 'em on, mother, they say they'd as soon sleep on the straw in the barn as anywheres else."

"There's plenty to eat, such as it is, but Ruth Mary'll have it all to do. I can't be on my feet." Mrs. Tully spoke in a depressed tone, but to her no less than to her husband was this little break welcome in the monotony of their life in the hills, even though it brought with it a more vivid conscious-ness of the family circumstances, and a review of them in the light of former standards of comfort and gentility: for Mrs. Tully had been a woman of some social pretensions, in the small Eastern village where she was born. To all that to her guests made the unique charm of her present home she had grown callous, if she had ever felt it at all, while dwelling with an incurable regret upon the neatly painted houses and fenced door-yards, the gatherings of women in their best clothes in primly furnished parlors on summer afternoons, the church-going, the passing in the street, and, more than all, the housekeeping conveniences she had been used to, accumulated through many years' occupancy of the same house.

"Seems as though I hadn't any ambition left," she often complained to her daughter. "There's nothin' here to do with, and nobody to do for. The most of the folks we ever see wouldn't know sour-dough bread from salt-risin', and as for dressin' up, I might keep the same clothes on from Fourth July till Christmas—your father'd never know."

But Ruth Mary was haunted by no fleshpots of the past. As she dressed the chickens and mixed the biscuit for supper, she paused often in her work and looked towards the high pastures with the pale brown lights and purple shadows on them, rolling away and rising towards the great tim-bered ridges, and these lifting here and there along their profiles a treeless peak or bare divide into the regions above vegetation. She had no misgiv-ings about her home. Fences would not have improved her father's vast lawn, to her mind, or white paint the low-browed front of his dwelling; nor did she feel the want of a stair-carpet and a parlor-organ. She was sure that they, the strangers, had never seen anything more lovely than her beloved river dancing down between the hills, tripping over rapids, wrinkling over sand-bars of its own spreading, and letting out its speed down the long reaches where the channel was deep.

About four o'clock she found leisure to stroll along the shore with Tommy, whose competitive energies as a fisherman had been stimulated by the advent of strange craftsmen with scientific-looking tackle. Tommy must forthwith show what native skill could do with a willow pole and grasshoppers for bait. But Ruth Mary's sense of propriety would by no means tolerate Tommy's intruding his company upon the strangers, and to frustrate any rash, gregarious impulses on his part she judged it best to keep him in sight.

Tommy knew of a deep pool under the willows which he could whip, unseen, in the shady hours of the afternoon. Thither he led Ruth Mary, leaving her seated upon the bank above him lest she should be tempted to talk, and so interfere with his sport. The moments went by in silence, broken only by the river; Ruth Mary happy on the high bank in the sun,

Tommy happy by the shady pool below, and now and then slapping a lively trout upon the stones. Across the river two Chinamen were washing gravel in a rude miner's cradle, paddling about on the river's brink, and anon staggering down from the gravel bank above, with large square kerosene cans filled with pay dirt balanced on either end of a pole across their meagre shoulders. Bare-headed, in their loose garments, with their pottering movements and wrinkled faces shining with heat, they looked like two weird, unrevered old women working out some dismal penance. High up in the sky the great black buzzards sailed and sailed on slanting wing; the wood doves coo-oo-ed from the willow thickets that gathered the sunlight close to the water's edge. A few horses and cattle moved like specks upon the sides of the hills, cropping the bunchgrass, but the greater herds had been driven up into the high pastures where the snow falls early; and all these lower hills were bare of life, unless one might fancy that the far-off processions of pines against the sky, marching up the northern sides of the divides, had a solemn personality, going up like priests to a sacrifice, or that the restless river, flowing through the midst of all and bearing the light of the white noonday sky deep into the bosom of the darkest hills, had a soul as well as a voice. In its sparkle and ever-changing motion it was like a child among its elders at play. The hills seemed to watch it, and the great cloud-heads as they looked down between the parting summits, and the three tall pines, standing about a young bird's flight from each other by the shore and mingling their fitful crooning with the river's babble.

It is pleasant to think of Ruth Mary, sitting high above the river, in the peaceful afternoon, surrounded by the inanimate life that to her brought the fullness of companionship and left no room for vain cravings; the shadow creeping upward over her hands folded in her lap, the light resting on her girlish face and meek, smooth hair. For this was during that unquestioning time of content which may not always last, even in a life as safe and as easily predicted as hers. But even now this silent communion was interrupted by the appearance of one of Tommy's rivals. It was the young man whose comrades called him Kirk, who came along the shore, stooping under the willow boughs and scattering all their shadows lightly traced on the stones below. He held his fishing-rod, couched like a lance, in one hand, and a string of gleaming fish in the other.

Tommy, with practiced eye, rapidly counted them and saw with chagrin that he was outnumbered, but another look satisfied him that the stranger's catch was nearly all "white-fish" instead of trout. He caressed his own dappled beauties complacently.

Kirkwood stopped and looked at them; he was evidently impressed by Tommy's superior luck.

"Those are big fellows," he said; "did you catch them?"

"You don't suppose *she* did?" said Tommy, with a jerk of his head towards Ruth Mary.

Kirkwood looked up and smiled, seeing the young girl on her sunny perch. The smile lingered pleasantly in his eyes as he seated himself on the stones—deliberately, as if he meant to stay.

Tommy watched him while he made himself comfortable, taking from his pocket a short briar-wood pipe and a bag of tobacco, leisurely filling the pipe and lighting it with a wax match held in the hollow of his hands—apparently from habit, for there was no wind. He did not seem to mind in the least that his legs were wet and that his trout were nearly all white-fish. He was evidently a person of happy resources, and a joy-compelling temperament that could find virtue in white-fish if it couldn't get trout. He began to talk to Tommy, not without an amused consciousness of Tommy's silent partner on the bank above, nor without an occasional glance up at the maidenly head serenely exalted in the sunlight. Nor did Ruth Mary fail to respond, with her down-bent looks, as simply and unawares as the clouds turning their bright side to the sun.

Tommy, on his part, was stoutly withholding, in words, the admiration his eyes could not help showing, of the strange fisherman's tools. He cautiously felt the weight of the ringed and polished rod, and snapped it lightly over the water; he was permitted to examine the book of flies and to handle the reel, things in themselves fascinating, but to Tommy's mind merely a hindrance and a snare to the understanding in the real business of catching fish. Still, he admitted, where a man could take a whole day all to himself like that, without fear of being called off at any moment by the women on some frivolous household errand, he might afford to potter with such things. Tommy kept the conservative attitude of native experience and skill towards foreign innovation.

"If Joe Enselman was here," he said, "I bet he could ketch more fish in half 'n hour, with a pole like this o' mine and a han'ful o' 'hoppers, than any of you can in a whole week o' fishing with them fancy things."

"Oh, Tommy!" Ruth Mary expostulated, looking distressed.

"Who is this famous fisherman?" Kirkwood asked, smiling at Tommy's boast.

"Oh, he's a feller I know. He's a packer, and he owns ha'f o' father's stock. He's goin' to marry our Sis soon's he gits back from Sheep Mountain, and then he'll be my brother." Tommy had been a little reckless in his desire for the distinction of a personal claim on the hero of his boyish heart. He was even conscious of this himself, as he glanced up at his sister.

Kirkwood's eyes involuntarily followed Tommy's. He withdrew them at once, but not before he saw the troubled blush that reddened the girl's averted face. It struck him, though he was not deeply versed in blushes, that it was not quite the expression of happy, maidenly consciousness, when the name of a lover is unexpectedly spoken.

It was the first time in her life that Ruth Mary had ever blushed at the name of Joe Enselman. She could not understand why it should pain her to have this young stranger hear of him in his relation to herself.

Before her blush had faded, Kirkwood had dismissed the subject of Ruth Mary's engagement, with the careless reflection that Enselman was probably not the right man, but that the primitive laws which decide such haphazard unions doubtless provided the necessary hardihood of temperament wherewith to meet their exigencies. She was a nice little girl, but possibly she was not so sensitive as she looked.

His pipe had gone out, and after relighting it, he showed Tommy the gayly pictured paper match-box from Havana, which opened with a spring, and disclosed the matches lying in a little drawer within. Tommy's wistful eyes, as he returned the box, prompted Kirkwood to make prudent search in his pockets for a second box of matches before presenting Tommy with the one his eyes coveted. Finding himself secure against want in the immediate future, he gave himself up to the mild amusement of watching Tommy with his new acquisition.

Tommy could not resist lighting one of the little tapers, which burned in the sunlight with a still, clear flame like a fairy candle. Then a second one was sacrificed. By this time the attraction had proved strong enough to bring Ruth Mary down from her high seat in the sun. She looked scarcely less a child than Tommy, as, with her face close to his, she watched the pale flame flower wasting its waxen stem. Then she must needs light one herself and hold it, with a little fixed smile on her face, till the flame crept down and warmed her finger-tips.

"There," she said, putting it out with a breath, "don't let us burn any more. It's too bad to waste 'em in the daylight."

"We will burn one more," said Kirkwood, "not for amusement, but for information." And while he whittled a piece of driftwood into the shape of a boat, he told Ruth Mary how the Hindoo maidens set their lighted lamps afloat at night on the Ganges, and watch them perilously voyaging, to learn, by the fate of the traveling flame, the safety of their absent lovers.

He told it simply and gravely, as he might have described some fact in natural history, for he rightly guessed that this little seed of sentiment fell on virgin soil. According to Tommy, Ruth Mary was betrothed and soon to be a wife, but Kirkwood was curiously sure that as yet she knew not love, nor even fancy. Nor had he any deliberate intention of tampering with her inexperience. He spoke of the lamps on the Ganges because they came into his mind while Ruth Mary was bending over the wasting match flame; any hesitation he might have had about introducing so delicate a topic was conquered by an idle fancy that he would like to observe its effect upon her almost pathetic innocence.

While he talked, interrupting himself as his whittling absorbed him, but always conscious of her eyes upon his face, the boat took shape in his hands. Tommy had failed to catch the connection between Hindoo girls and boat-making, but was satisfied with watching Kirkwood's skillful fingers, without paying much heed to his words. The stranger had, too, a wonderful knife, with tools concealed in its handle, with one of which he bored a hole for the mast. In the top of the mast he fixed a wax taper upright and steady for the voyage.

Ruth Mary's cheeks grew red, as she suddenly perceived the intention of Kirkwood's whittling.

"Now," he said, steadying the boat on the shallow ripple, "before we light our beacon you must think of some one you care for, who is away. Perhaps Tommy's friend, on Sheep Mountain?" he ventured softly, glancing at Ruth Mary.

The color in her cheeks deepened, and again Kirkwood fancied it was not a happy confusion that covered her downcast face.

"No?" he questioned, as Ruth Mary did not speak; "that is too serious, perhaps. Well, then, make a little wish, and if the light is still alive when the boat passes that rock—the flat one with two stones on top—the wish will come true. But you must have faith, you know."

Ruth Mary looked at Kirkwood, the picture of faith in her sweet seriousness. His heart smote him a little, but he met her wide-eyed gaze with a gravity equal to her own.

"I would rather not wish for myself," she said, "but I will wish something for you, if you want me to."

"That is very kind of you. Am I to know what it is to be?"

"Oh yes. You must tell me what to wish."

"That is easily done," said Kirkwood gayly. "Wish that I may come back some other day, and sit here with you and Tommy by the river."

It was impossible not to see that Ruth Mary was blushing again. But she answered him with a gentle courtesy that rebuked the foolish blush: "That will be wishing for us all."

"Shall we light up then, and set her afloat?"

"I've made a wish," shouted Tommy; "I've wished Joe Enselman would bring me an Injun pony: a good one that won't buck!"

"You must keep your wish for the next trip. This ship is freighted deep enough already. Off she goes then, and good luck to the wish," said Kirkwood, as the current took the boat, with the light at its peak burning clearly, and swept it away. The pretty plaything dipped and danced a moment, while the light wavered but still lived. Then a breath of wind shook the willows, and the light was gone.

"Now it's my turn," Tommy exclaimed, wasting no sentiment on another's failure. He rushed down the bank and into the shallow water to catch the wishing-boat before it drifted away.

"All the same I'm coming back again," said Kirkwood, looking at Ruth Mary.

Tommy's wish fared no better than his sister's, but he bore up briskly, declaring it was "all foolishness anyway," and accused Kirkwood of having "just made it up for fun."

Kirkwood only laughed, and, ignoring Tommy, said to Ruth Mary, "The game was hardly worth the candle, was it?"

"Was it a game?" she asked. "I thought you meant it for true."

"Oh no," he said; "when we try it in earnest we must find a smoother river and a stronger light. Besides, you know, I'm coming back."

Ruth Mary kept her eyes upon his face, still questioning his seriousness, but its quick changes of expression baffled while fascinating her. She could not have told whether she thought him handsome or not, but she had a desire to look at him all the time.

Suddenly her household duties recurred to her, and, refusing the help of Kirkwood's hand, she sprang up the bank and hurried back to the house. Kirkwood could see her head above the wild-rose thickets as she went along the high path by the shore. He was more sure than ever that Enselman was not the right man.

At supper Ruth Mary waited on the strangers in silence, while Angy kept the cats and dogs "corraled," as her father called it, in the shed, that their impetuous appetites might not disturb the feast.

Mr. Tully stood in the doorway and talked with his guests while they ate, and Mrs. Tully, with the little two-year-old in her lap, rocked in the large rocking-chair and sighed apologetically between her promptings of Ruth Mary's attendance on the table.

Tommy hung about in a state of complete infatuation with the person and conversation of his former rival. He was even beginning to waver in his allegiance to his absent hero, especially as the wish about the Indian pony had not come true.

During the family meal the young men sat outside in the shed-room, and smoked and lazily talked together. Their words reached the silent group at the table. Kirkwood's companions were deriding him as a recreant sportsman. He puffed his short-stemmed pipe and looked at them tranquilly. He was not dissatisfied with his share of the day's pleasure.

When Mr. Tully had finished his supper, he took the young men down to the beach to look at his boat. Kirkwood had pointed it out to his comrades, where it lay moored under the bank, and ventured the opinion of a boating man that it had not been built in the mountains. But there he had generalized too rashly.

"I built her myself," said Mr. Tully; "rip-sawed the lumber up here. My young ones are as handy with her!" he boasted cheerfully, warmed by the admiration his work called forth. "You'd never believe, to see 'em knocking about in her, they hadn't the first one of 'em ever smelt salt water. Ruth Mary now, the oldest of 'em, is as much to home in that boat as she is on a hoss—and that's sayin' enough. She looks quiet, but she's got as firm a seat and as light a hand as any cow-boy that ever put leg over a cayuse."

Mr. Tully, on being questioned, admitted willingly that he was an Eastern man—a Down-East lumberman and boat-builder. He couldn't say just why he'd come West. Got restless, and his wife's health was always poor back there. He had mined it some and had had considerable luck—cleaned up several thousands, the summer of '63, at Junction Bar. Put it in a saw-mill and got burned out. Then he took up this cattle range and went into stock, in partnership with a young fellow from Montana, named Enselman. They expected to make a good thing of it, but it was a long ways from anywheres; and for months of the year they couldn't do any teaming. Had no way out except by the horseback trail. The women found it lonesome. In winter no team could get up that grade in the canon they call the "freeze-out," even if they could cross the river, on account of the ice; and from April to August the river was up so you couldn't ford.

All this in the intervals of business, for Mr. Tully, in his circuitous way, was agreeing to build a boat for the engineers, after the model of his own. He would have to go down to the camp at Moor's Bridge to build it, he said, for suitable lumber could not be procured so far up the river, except at great expense. It would take him better'n a month, anyhow, and he didn't know what his women-folks would say to having him so long away. He would see about it.

The four men sauntered up the path from the shore, Tommy bringing up the rear with the little black-and-tan terrier. In default of a word from his master, Tommy tried to make friends with the dog, but the latter, wide awake and suspicious after dozing under the wagon all the afternoon, would none of him. Possibly he divined that Tommy's attentions were not wholly disinterested.

The family assembled for the evening in the shed-room. The women were silent, for the talk was confined to masculine topics, such as the quality of the placer claims up the river, the timber, the hunting, the progress and prospects of the new railroad. Tommy, keeping himself forcibly awake, was seeing two Kirkwoods where there was but one. The terrier had taken shelter between Kirkwood's knees, after trying conclusions with the mother of the kittens—a cat of large experience and a reserved disposition, with only one ear, but in full possession of her faculties.

Betimes the young men arose and said good-night. Mr. Tully was loath to have the evening, with its rare opportunity for conversation, brought to a close, but he was too modest a host to press his company upon his guests. He went with them to their bed, on the clean straw in the barn, and if good wishes could soften pillows the travelers would have slept sumptuously. They did not know, in fact, how they slept, but woke, strong and joyous over the beauty of the morning on the hills, and the prospect of continuing their journey.

They parted from the family at the ranch with a light-hearted promise to stop again on their way down the river. When they would return they were gayly uncertain—it might be ten days, it might be two weeks. It was a promise that nestled with delusive sweetness in Ruth Mary's thoughts, as she went silently about her work. She was helpful in all ways, and very gentle with the children, but she lingered more hours dreaming by the river, and often at twilight she climbed the hill back of the cabin and sat there alone, her cheek in the hollow of her hand, until the great planes of distance were lost, and all the hills drew together in one dark profile against the sky.

*　　*　　*　　*　　*

Mrs. Tully had been intending to spare Ruth Mary for a journey to town, on some errands of a feminine nature which could not be intrusted to Mr. Tully's larger but less discriminating judgment. Ruth Mary had never before been known to trifle with an opportunity of this kind. Her rides to town had been the one excitement of her life; looked forward to with eagerness and discussed with tireless interest for many days afterwards. But now she hung back with an unaccountable apathy, and made excuses for postponing the ride from day to day, until the business became too pressing to be longer neglected. She set off one morning at daybreak, following the horseback trail, around the steep and sliding bluffs high above the river, or across beds of broken lava rock—arrested avalanches from the slowly crumbling cliffs which crowned the bluff—or picking her way at a soft-footed pace through the thickets of the river bottoms. In such a low and sheltered spot, scarcely four feet above the river, she found the engineers' camp, a group of white tents shining among the willows. She keenly noted its location and surroundings. The broken timbers of the old bridge projected from the bank a short distance above the camp; a piece of weather-stained canvas stretched over them formed a kind of awning shading the rocks below, where the Chinese cook of the camp sat impassively fishing. The camp had a deserted appearance, for the men were all at work, tunneling the hill half a mile lower down. Her errands kept her so late that she was obliged to stay over night at the house of a friend of her father's, who owned a fruit ranch near the town. They were prosperous, talkative people, who loudly pitied the isolation of the family in the upper valley.

Ruth Mary reached home about noon the next day, tired and several shades more deeply sunburned, to find that she had passed the engineers, without knowing it, on their way down the river by the wagon road on the other side. They had stopped over night at the ranch and made an early start that morning. Ruth Mary was obliged to listen to enthusiastic reminiscences, from each member of the family, of the visit she had missed.

This was the last social event of the year. The willow copses turned yellow and leaf-bare; the scarlet hips of the rosebushes looked as if tiny finger-tips had left their prints upon them. The wreaths of wild clematis faded ashen gray, and were scattered by the winds. The wood dove's cooing no longer sounded at twilight in the leafless thickets. They had gone down the river and the wild duck with them.

But the voice of the river, rising with the autumn rains, was loud on the bar; the sky was hung with clouds that hid the hilltops or trailed their ragged pennants below the summits. The mist lay cold on the river; it rose with the sun, dissolving in soft haze that dulled the sunshine, and at night, descending, shrouded the dark, hoarse water without stilling its lament. Then the first snow fell, and ghostly companies of deer came out upon the hills, or filed silently down the draws of the canons at morning and evening. The cattle had come down from the mountain pastures, and at night congregated about the buildings with deep breathings and sighings; the river murmured in its fretted channel; now and then the yelp of a hungry coyote sounded from the hills.

The young men had said, among their light and pleasant sayings, that they would like to come up again to the hills when the snow fell, and get a shot at the deer; but they did not come, though often Ruth Mary stood on the bank and looked across the swollen ford, and listened for the echo of wheels among the hills.

About the 1st of November Mr. Tully went down to the camp at Moor's Bridge to build the engineers' boat. The women were now alone at the ranch, but Joe Enselman's return was daily expected. Mr. Tully, always cheerful, had been confident that he would be home by the 5th.

The 5th of November and the 10th passed, but Enselman had not returned. On the 12th, in the midst of a heavy fall of snow, his pack animals were driven in by another man, a stranger to the women at the ranch, who said that Enselman had changed his mind suddenly about coming home that fall, and decided to go to Montana and "prove up" on his ranch there.

Mr. Tully's work was finished before the second week of December. On his return to the ranch he brought with him a great brown paper bundle, which the children opened by the cabin fire on the joyous evening of his arrival. There were back numbers of the illustrated magazines and papers, stray copies of which now and then had drifted into the hands of the voracious young readers in the cabin. There were a few novels, selected by Kirkwood from the camp library with especial reference to Ruth Mary. For Tommy there was a duplicate of the wonderful pocket-knife that he had envied Kirkwood. Angy was remembered with a little music-box, which played "Willie, we have missed you" with a plaintive iteration that brought the sensitive tears to Ruth Mary's eyes; and for Ruth Mary herself there was a lace pin of hammered gold.

"He said it must be your wedding present from him, as you'd be married likely before he saw you again," Mr. Tully said, with innocent pride in the gift with which his daughter had been honored.

"Who said that?" Ruth Mary asked.

"Why, Mr. Kirkwood said it. He's the boss one of the whole lot to my thinkin'. He's got that way with him some folks has! We had some real good talks, evenings, down on the rocks under the old bridge—I told him about you and Enselman—"

"Father, I wish you hadn't done that." The protest in Ruth Mary's voice was stronger than her words.

She had become slightly pale when Kirkwood's name was mentioned, but now, as she held out the box with the trinket in it, a deep blush covered her face.

"I cannot take it, father. Not with that message. He can wait till I am married before he sends me his wedding present."

To her father's amazement, she burst into tears and went out into the shed-room, leaving Kirkwood's ill-timed gift in his hands.

"What in all conscience' sake's got into her?" he demanded of his wife, "to take offense at a little thing like that! She didn't use to be so techy."

Mrs. Tully nodded her head at him sagely and glanced at the children, a hint that she understood Ruth Mary's state of mind, but could not explain before them.

At bedtime, the father and mother being alone together, Mrs. Tully revealed the cause of her daughter's sensitiveness, according to her theory of it. "She's put out because Joe Enselman chose to wait till spring before marryin', and went off to Montany instead of comin' home as he said he would."

"Sho, sho!" said Mr. Tully. "That don't seem like Ruth Mary. She ain't in any such a hurry as all that comes to. I've had it on my mind lately that she took it a little too easy."

"You'll see," said the mother. "*She* ain't in any hurry, but she likes *him* to be. She feels's if he thought more of money-makin' than he does of her. She's like all girls. She won't use her reason and see it's all for her in the end he's doin' it."

"Why didn't you tell her 'twas my plan, his goin' to Montany this fall? He wouldn't listen to it nohow then. He'd rather lose his ranch than wait any longer for Sis, so he said; but I guess he's seen the sense of what I told him. 'Ruth Mary ain't a-goin' to run away,' I says, 'even if ye don't prove up on her this fall.' You ought to 'a' told her, mother, 'twas my proposition."

"I told her that and more too. I told her it showed he'd make a good provider. She looked at me solemn as a graven image all the time I was talkin' and not a word out of her. But that's Ruth Mary. I never said the child was sullen, but she is just like your sister Ruth—the more she feels, the less she talks."

"Well," said Mr. Tully, "that's all right, if that's it. That'll all straighten out with time. It was natural perhaps she should fire up at the talk about marryin' if she felt the bridegroom was hangin' back. Why, Joe—he'd eat the dirt she treads on, if he couldn't make her like him no other way! He's most too foolish about her, to my thinkin'. That's what took me so by surprise when word come back he'd gone to Montany after all; I didn't expect anything so sensible of him."

" 'Twas a reg'lar man's piece o' work anyhow," said Mrs. Tully disconsolately.

"And you'll be sorry for it, I'm afraid. I never knew any good come of puttin' off a marriage, where everything was suitable, just for a few hundred acres of wild land, more or less."

"No use your worryin'," said Mr. Tully. "Young folks always has their little troubles before they settle down—besides, what sort of a marriage would it be if you or I could make it or break it?" But he bore himself with a deprecating tenderness towards his daughter, in whose affairs he had meddled, perhaps disastrously, as his better half feared.

*　　*　　*　　*　　*

The winters of Idaho are not long, even in the higher valleys. Close upon the cold footsteps of the retreating snows trooped the first wild flowers. The sun seemed to laugh in the cloudless sky. The children were let loose on the hills; their voices echoed the river's chime. Its waters, rising with the melting snows, no longer babbled childishly on their way; they shouted, and brawled, and tumbled over the bar, rolling huge pine trunks along as if they were sticks of kindling wood.

One cool May evening, Ruth Mary, climbing the path from the beach, saw there was a strange horse and two pack animals in the corral. She did not stop to look at them, but, quickly guessing who their owner must be, she went on to the house, her knees weak and trembling, her heart beating heavily. Her father met her at the door and detained her outside. She was prepared for his announcement. She knew that Joe Enselman had returned, and that the time was come for her to prove her new resolve, born of the winter's silent struggle.

"I thought I'd better have a few words with you, Ruthie, before you see him—to prepare your mind. Set down here." Mr. Tully took his daughter's hands in his own and held them while he talked.

"You thought it was queer Joe stayed away so long, didn't you?" Ruth Mary opened her lips to speak, but no words came. "Well, I did," said the father. "Though it was my plan first off. I might 'a' know'd it was something more 'n business that kep' him. Joe's had an accident. It happened to him just about the time he meant to 'a' started for home last fall. It broke him all up—made him feel like he didn't want to see any of us just then. He was goin' along a trail through the woods one dark night; he never knew what stunned him; must have been a twig or something struck him in the eye; he was giddy and crazy-like for a spell; his horse took him home. Well, he ain't got but one eye left, Joe ain't. There, Sis, I knew you'd feel bad. But he's well. It's hurt his looks some, but what's looks! We ain't any of us got any to brag on. Joe had some hopes at first he'd git to seein' again out of the eye that was hurt, and so he sent home his animals and put out for Salt Lake to show it to a doctor there; but it wan't any use. The eye's gone; and it doos seem as if for the time bein' some of Joe's grit had gone with it. He went up to Montany and tended to his business, but it was all like a dumb show and no heart in it. It's cut him pretty deep, through his bein' alone so long, perhaps, and thinkin' about how you'd feel. And then he's pestered in his mind about marryin'. He feels he's got no claim to you now. Says it ain't fair to ask a young girl that's likely to have plenty good chances to tie up to what's left of him. I wanted you should know about this before you go inside. It might hurt him some to see a change in your face when you look at him first. As to his givin' you your word back, that you'll settle between yourselves; but, however you fix it, I guess you'll make it as easy as you can for Joe. I don' know as ever I see a big strappin' fellow so put down."

Mr. Tully had waited, between his short and troubled sentences, for some response from Ruth Mary, but she was still silent. Her hands felt cold in his. As he released them she leaned suddenly forward and hid her face against his shoulder. She shivered and her breast heaved, but she was not weeping.

"There, there!" said Mr. Tully, stroking her head clumsily with his large hand. "I've made a botch of it. I'd ought to 'a' let your mother told ye."

She pressed closer to him, and wrapped her arms around him without speaking.

"I expect I better go in now," he said gently, putting her away from him. "Will you come along o' me, or do you want to git a little quieter first?"

"You go in," Ruth Mary whispered. "I'll come soon."

It was not long before she followed her father into the house. No one was surprised to see her white and tremulous. She seemed to know where Enselman sat without raising her eyes; neither did he venture to look at her, as she came to him, and stooping forward, laid her little cold hands on his.

"I'm glad you've come back," she said. Then sinking down suddenly on the floor at his feet, she threw her apron over her head and sobbed aloud.

The father and mother wept too. Joe sat still, with a great and bitter longing in his smitten countenance, but did not dare to comfort her.

"Pick her up, Joe," said Mr. Tully.

"Take hold of her, man, and show her you've got a whole heart if you ain't got but one eye."

It was understood, as Ruth Mary meant that it should be, without more words, that Enselman's misfortune would make no difference in their old relation. The difference it had made in that new resolve born of the winter's struggle she told to no one; for to no one had she confided her resolve.

*   *   *   *   *

Joe stayed two weeks at the ranch, and was comforted into a semblance of his former hardy cheerfulness. But Ruth Mary knew that he was not happy. One evening he asked her to go with him down the high shore path. He told her that he was going to town the next day on business that might keep him absent about a fortnight, and entreated her to think well of her promise to him, for that on his return he should expect its fulfillment. For God's sake he begged her to let no pity for his misfortune blind her to the true nature of her feeling for him. He held her close to his heart and kissed her many times. Did she love him so—and so?—he asked. Ruth Mary, trembling, said she did not know. How could she help knowing? he demanded passionately. Had her thoughts been with him all winter, as his had been with her? Had she looked up the river towards the hills where he was staying so long and wished for him, as he had gazed southward into the valleys many and many a day, longing for the sweet blue eyes of his little girl so far away?

Alas, Ruth Mary! She gazed almost wildly into his stricken face, distorted by the anguish of his great love and his great dread. She wished that she were dead. There seemed no other way out of her trouble.

The next morning, before she was dressed, Enselman rode away, and her father went with him.

She was alone, now, in the midst of the hills she loved—alone as she would never be again. She foresaw that she would not have the strength to lay that last blow upon her faithful old friend—the crushing blow that perfect truth demanded. Her tenderness was greater than her truth.

* * * * *

The river was now swollen to its greatest volume. Its voice, that had been the babble of a child and the tumult of a boy, was now deep and heavy like the chest notes of a strong man. Instead of the sparkling ripple on the bar, there was a continuous roar of yellow, turbid water that could be heard a mile away. There had been no fording for six weeks, nor would there be again until late summer. The useless boat lay in the shallow wash that filled the deep cut among the willows. The white sand beach was gone; heavy waves swirled past the banks and sent their eddies up into the channels of the hills to meet the streams of melted snow. Thunder clouds chased each other about the mountains, or met in sudden downfalls of rain.

One sultry noon, when the sun had come out hot on the hills after a wet morning, Ruth Mary, at work in the shed-room, heard a sound that drove the color from her cheek. She ran out and looked up the river, listening to a distant but ever increasing roar which could be heard above the incessant laboring of the waters over the bar. Above the summit of Sheep Mountain, as it seemed, a huge turban-shaped cloud had rolled itself up, and from its central folds was discharging gray sheets of water that veered and slanted with the wind, but were always distinct in their density against the rain-charged atmosphere. How far away the floods were descending she did not know; but that they were coming in a huge wall of water, overtaking and swallowing up the river's current, she was as sure as that she had been bred in the mountains.

Bare-headed, bare-armed as she was, without a backward look, she ran down the hill to the place where the boat was moored. Tommy was there, sitting in the boat and making the shallow water splash as he rocked from side to side.

"Get out, Tommy, and let me have her, quick!" Ruth Mary called to him.

Tommy looked at her stolidly and kept on rocking. "What you want with her?" he asked.

"Come out, for mercy's sake! Don't you *hear* it? There's a cloud-burst on the mountain."

Tommy listened. He did hear it, but he did not stir. "It'll be a bully thing to see when it comes. What you doin'? You act like you was crazy," he exclaimed, as Ruth Mary waded through the water and got into the boat.

"Tommy, you will kill me if you stop to talk! Don't you know the camp at Moor's Bridge? Go home and tell mother I've gone to give 'em warning."

Tommy was instantly sobered. "I'm going with you," he said. "You can't handle her alone in that current."

Ruth Mary, wild with the delay, every second of which might be the price of precious lives, seized Tommy in her arms, hugged him close and kissed him, and by main strength rolled him out into the water. He grasped the gunwale with both hands. "You're going to be drowned," he shrieked, as if already she were far away. She pushed off his hands and shot out into the current.

"Don't cry, Tommy, I'll get there somehow," she called back to him. She could see nothing for the first few minutes of her journey but his little wet, dismal figure toiling, sobbing, up the hill. It hurt her to have had to be rough with him. But all the while she sat upright with her eyes on the current, plying her paddle right and left, as rocks and driftwood and eddies were passed. She heard it coming, that distant roar from the hills, and prayed with beating heart that the wild current might carry her faster—faster—past the draggled willow copses—past the beds of black lava rock, and the bluffs with their patches of green moss livid in the sunshine—hurling along, past glimpses of the well-known trail she had followed dreamily on those peaceful rides she might never take again. The thought did not trouble her, only the fear that she might be overtaken before she reached the camp. For the waters were coming—or was it the wind that brought that dread sound so near! She dared not look round lest she should see, through the gates of the canon, the black lifted head of the great wave, devouring the river behind her. How it would come swooping down, between those high narrow walls of rock, her heart stood still to think of. If the hills would but open and let it loose, over the empty pastures—if the river would only hurry, hurry, hurry! She whispered the word to herself with frantic repetition, and the oncoming roar behind her answered her whisper of fear with its awful intoning.

She trembled with joy as the canon walls lowered and fell apart, and she saw the blessed plains, the low green flats and the willows, and the white tents of the camp, safe in the sunshine. Now if she be given but one moment's grace to swing into the bank! The roar behind her made her faint as she listened. For the first time she turned and looked back, and the cry of her despair went up and was lost, as boat and message and messenger were lost—gone utterly, gorged at one leap by the senseless flood.

* * * * *

At half past five o'clock that afternoon the men of the camp filed out of the tunnel, along the new road-bed, with the low sunlight in their faces. It was "Saturday night," and the whole force was in good humor. As they tramped gayly along, tools and instruments glinting in the sun, word went down the line that something unusual had been going on by the river. There seemed to have been a wild uprising of its waters since they saw it last. Then a shout from those ahead proclaimed the disaster at the bridge. The Chinese cook, crouched among the rocks high up under the bluff, where he had fled for safety when he heard the waters coming, rushed down to them with wild wavings and gabblings, to tell them of a catastrophe that was best described by its results. A few provisions were left them, stored in a magazine under a rock on the hillside. They cooked their supper with the splinters of the ruined blacksmith's hut. After supper, in the clear, pink evening light, they wandered about on the slippery rocks, seeking whatever fragments of their camp equipage the flood might have left them. Everything had been swept away, and tons of mud and gravel covered the little green meadow where their tents had stood. Kirkwood, straying on ahead of his comrades, came to the rocks below the bridge timbers, from which the awning had been torn away. The wet rocks glistened in the light, but there was a whiter gleam which caught his eye. He stooped and crawled under the timbers anchored in the bank, until he came to the spot of whiteness. Was this that fair young girl from the hills, dragged here by the waters in their cruel orgy, and then hidden by them as if in shame of their work? Kirkwood recognized the simple features, the meek eyes, wide open in the searching light. The mud that filled her garments had spared the pure young face. Kirkwood gazed into it reverently, but the passionate sacrifice, the useless warning, were sealed from him. She could not tell him why she was there.

The three young men watched in turn, that night, by the little motionless heap covered with Kirkwood's coat. Kirkwood was very sad about Ruth Mary, yet he slept when his watch was over.

In the morning they nailed together some boards into the shape of a long box. There was not a boat left on the river; fording was impossible. They could only take her home by the trail. So once more Ruth Mary traveled that winding path, high in the sunlight or low in the shade of the shore. A log of driftwood, left by the great wave, slung on one side of a mule's pack saddle, balanced the rude coffin on the other. No one meeting the three engineers and their pack-mule filing down the trail would have known that they were a funeral procession; but they were heavy-hearted as they rode along, and Kirkwood would fain it had not been his part to ride ahead and prepare the family at the ranch for their child's coming.

The mother, with Tommy and Angy hiding their faces against her, stood on the hill and watched for it, and broke into cries as the mule with its burden came in sight.

Kirkwood walked with them down the hill to meet it. His comrades dismounted, and the three young men, with heads uncovered, carried the coffin over the hill and set it down in the shed-room. Then Tommy, in a burst of childish grief, made them know that this piteous sacrifice had been for them.

The tunnel made its way through the hill, the sinuous road-bed wound up the valley, new camps were built along its course; but when the young men sat together of an evening and looked at the hills in the strange pink light, a spell of quietness rested upon them which no one tried to explain.

*   *   *   *   *

The railroad has been built these two years. Every summer brings tourists up into the Bear River valley. They look with delight upon the mountain stream, bounding down between the hills with the brightness of the morning on its breast.

"There should be an idyl or a legend belonging to it," a pretty, dark-eyed girl with a Boston accent said to Kirkwood, one moonlight evening late in summer when the river was low, as they drifted softly down between its dim shores. "Poor little Bear River! did nothing human ever happen near you to give you a right to a prettier name?"

The river did not answer as it rippled over the bar, nor did Kirkwood speak for it; but the wood dove's melancholy tremolo came from the misty willows by the shore, and in some suddenly illumined place in his memory he saw Ruth Mary, sitting on the high bank in the peaceful afternoon, the sunshine resting on her smooth, fair hair, the shadow lending its softness to her shy, down-bent face.

The pity of it, when he thinks of it sometimes, seems to him more than he can bear. Yet if Ruth Mary had still been there at the ranch on the hills, she would have been, to him, only "that nice little girl of Tully's who married the one-eyed packer."

THE RAPTURE OF HETTY

The dance was set for Christmas night at Walling's, a horse-ranch where there were women, situated in a high, watered valley shut in by foot-hills, sixteen miles from the nearest town. The cabin with its roof of shakes, the sheds and corrals, can be seen from any divide between Packer's ferry and the Fayette.

The "boys" had been generally invited, with one exception to the usual company. The youngest of the sons of Basset, a pastoral and nomadic house, was socially under a cloud, on the charge of having been "too handy with the frying-pan brand."

The charge could not be substantiated, but the boy's name had been roughly handled in those wide, loosely defined circles of the range where the force of private judgment makes up for the weakness of the law, in dealing with crimes that are difficult of detection and uncertain of punishment. He that has obliterated his neighbor's brand or misapplied his own, is held as, in the age of tribal government and ownership, was held the remover of his neighbor's landmarks. A word goes forth against him potent as the levitical curse, and all the people say amen.

As society's first public and pointed rejection of him the slight had rankled with the son of Basset, and grievously it wore on him that Hetty Rhodes was going, with the man who had been his earliest and most persistent accuser: Hetty, prettiest of all the bunch-grass belles, who never reproached nor quarreled, but judged people with her smile and let them go. He had not complained, though he had her promise—one of her promises—nor asked a hearing in his own defense. The sons of Basset were many and poor; their stock had dwindled upon the range; her men-folk condemned him, and Hetty believed, or seemed to believe, as the others.

Had she forgotten the night when two men's horses stood at her father's fence—the Basset boy's and that of him who was afterward his accuser; and the other's horse was unhitched when the evening was but half spent, and furiously ridden away, while the Basset boy's stood at the rails till close upon midnight? Had the coincidence escaped her that from this night, of one man's rage and another's bliss, the ugly charge had dated? Of these things a girl may not testify.

They met in town on the Saturday before the dance, Hetty buying her dancing-shoes at the back of the store, where the shoe-cases framed in a snug little alcove for the exhibition of a "fit." The boy, in his belled spurs and "shaps" of goat-hide, was lounging disconsolate and sulky against one of the front counters; she wore a striped ulster, an enchanted garment his arm had pressed, and a pink crocheted tam-o'-shanter cocked bewitchingly over her dark eyes.

Her hair was ruffled, her cheeks were red, with the wind she had faced for two hours on the spring-seat of her father's "dead axe" wagon. Critical feminine eyes might have found her a trifle blowzy; the sick-hearted Basset boy looked once—he dared not look again.

Hetty coquetted with her partner in the shoe bargain, a curly-headed young Hebrew, who flattered her familiarly and talked as if he had known her from a child, but always with an eye to business. She stood, holding back her skirts and rocking her instep from right to left, while she considered the effect of the new style; patent-leather foxings and tan-cloth tops, and heels that came under the middle of her foot, and narrow toes with tips of stamped leather;—but what a price! More than a third of her chicken-money gone for that one fancy's satisfaction. But who can know the joy of a really distinguished choice in shoe-leather like one who in her childhood has trotted barefoot through the sage-brush and associated shoes only with cold weather or going to town? The Basset boy tried to fix his strained attention upon anything rather than upon that tone of high jocosity between Hetty and the shiny-haired clerk. He tried to summon his own self-respect and leave the place.

What was the tax, he inquired, on those neck-handkerchiefs; and he pointed with the loaded butt of his braided leather quirt to a row of dainty silk mufflers, signaling custom from a cord stretched above the gentlemen's-furnishing counter.

The clerk explained that the goods in question were first class, all silk, brocaded, and of an extra size. Plainly he expected that a casual mention of the price would cool the inexperienced customer's curiosity, especially as the colors displayed in the handkerchiefs were not those commonly affected by the cow-boy cult. The Basset boy threw down his last half-eagle and carelessly called for the one with a blue border. The delicate "baby blue" attracted him by its perishability, its suggestion of impossible refinements beyond the soilure and dust of his own grimy circumstances. Yet he pocketed his purchase as though it had been any common thing, not to show his pride in it before the patronizing salesman.

He waited foolishly for Hetty, not knowing if she would even speak to him. When she came at last, loitering down the shop, with her eyes on the gay Christmas counters and her arms filled with bundles, he silently fell in behind her and followed her to her father's wagon, where he helped her unload her purchases.

"Been buying out the store?" he opened the conversation.

"Buying more than father'll want to pay for," she drawled, glancing at him sweetly. Those entoiling looks of Hetty's dark-lashed eyes had grown to a habit with her; even now the little Jewish salesman was smiling over his brief portion in them. Her own coolness made her careless, as children are in playing with fire.

"Here's some Christmas the old man won't have to pay for." A soft paper parcel was crushed into her hand.

"Who is going to pay for it, I'd like to know? If it's some of your doings, Jim Basset, I can't take it—so there!"

She thrust the package back upon him. He tore off the wrapper and let the wind carry his rejected token into the trampled mud and slush of the street.

Hetty screamed and pounced to the rescue. "What a shame! It's a beauty of a handkerchief. It must have cost a lot of money. I shan't let you use it so."

She shook it, and wiped away the spots from its delicate sheen, and folded it into its folds again.

"*I* don't want the thing." He spurned it fiercely.

"Then give it to some one else." She endeavored coquettishly to force it into his hands, or into the pockets of his coat. He could not withstand her thrilling little liberties in the face of all the street.

"I'll wear it Monday night," said he. "May be you think I won't be there?" he added hoarsely, for he had noted her look of surprise, mingled with an infuriating touch of pity. "You kin bank on it I'll be there."

Hetty toyed with the thought that after all it might be better that she should not go to the dance. There might be trouble, for certainly Jim Basset had looked as if he meant it when he had said he would be there; and Hetty knew the temper of the company, the male portion of it, too well to doubt what their attitude would be toward an inhibited guest who disputed the popular verdict, and claimed social privileges which it had been agreed that he had forfeited. But it was never really in her mind to deny herself the excitement of going. She and her escort were among the first couples to cross the snowy pastures stretching between her father's claim and the lights of the lonely horse-ranch.

It was a cloudy night, the air soft, chill, and spring-like. Snow had fallen early and frozen upon the ground; the stockmen welcomed the "chinook wind" as the promise of a break in the hard weather. Shadows came out and played upon the pale slopes, as the riders rose and dropped past one long swell and another of dim country falling away like a ghostly land seeking a ghostly sea. And often Hetty looked back, fearing, yet half hoping, that the interdicted one might be on his way, among the dusky, straggling shapes behind.

The company was not large, nor, up to nine o'clock, particularly merry. The women were engaged in cooking supper, or were above in the roof-room brushing out their crimps by the light of an unshaded kerosene lamp, placed on the pine wash-stand which did duty as a dressing-table. The men's voices came jarringly through the loose boards of the floor from below.

About that hour arrived the unbidden guest, and like the others he had brought his "gun." He was stopped at the door and told that he could not come in among the girls to make trouble. He denied that he had come with any such intention. There were persons present—he mentioned no names—who were no more eligible, socially speaking, than himself, and he ranked himself low in saying so; where such as these could be admitted, he proposed to show that he could. He offered, in evidence of his good faith and peaceable intentions, to give up his gun; but on the condition that he be allowed one dance with the partner of his choosing, regardless of her previous engagements.

This unprecedented proposal was referred to the girls, who were charmed with its audacity. But none of them spoke up for the outcast till Hetty said she could not think what they were all afraid of; a dozen to one, and that one without his weapon! Then the other girls chimed in and added their timid suffrages.

There may have been some twinges of disappointment, there could hardly have been surprise, when the black sheep directed his choice without a look elsewhere to Hetty. She stood up, smiling but rather pale, and he rushed her to the head of the room, securing the most conspicuous place before his rival, who with his partner took the place of second couple opposite.

"Keep right on!" the fiddler chanted, in sonorous cadence to the music, as the last figure of the set ended with "Promenade all!" He swung into the air of the first figure again, smiling, with his cheek upon his instrument and his eyes upon the floor. Hetty fancied that his smile meant more than merely the artist's pleasure in the joy he evokes.

"*Keep* your places!" he shouted again, after the "Promenade all!" a second time had raised the dust and made the lamps flare, and lighted with smiles of sympathy the rugged faces of the elders ranged against the walls. The side couples dropped off exhausted, but the tops held the floor, and neither of the men was smiling.

The whimsical fiddler invented new figures, which he "called off" in time to his music, to vary the monotony of a quadrille with two couples missing.

The opposite girl was laughing hysterically; she could no longer dance nor stand. The rival gentleman looked about him for another partner. One girl jumped up, then, hesitating, sat down again. The music passed smoothly into a waltz, and Hetty and her bad boy kept the floor, regardless of shouts and protests warning the trespasser that his time was up and the game in other hands.

Three times they circled the room; they looked neither to right nor left; their eyes were upon each other. The men were all on their feet, the music playing madly. A group of half-scared girls was huddled, giggling and whispering, near the door of the dimly lighted shed-room. Into the midst of them Hetty's partner plunged, with his breathless, smiling dancer in his arms, passed into the dim outer place to the door where his horse stood saddled, and they were gone.

They crossed the little valley known as Seven Pines; they crashed through the thin ice of the creek; they rode double sixteen miles before daybreak, Hetty wrapped in her lover's "slicker," with the blue-bordered handkerchief, her only wedding-gift, tied over her blowing hair.

THE WATCHMAN

I

The far-Eastern company was counting its Western acres under water contracts. The acres were in first crops, waiting for the water. The water was dallying down its untried channel, searching the new dry earthbanks, seeping, prying, and insinuating sly, minute forces which multiplied and insisted tremendously the moment a rift had been made. And the orders were to "watch" and "puddle;" and the watchmen were as other men, and some of them doubtless remembered they were working for a company.

Travis, the black-eyed young lumberman from the upper Columbia, had been sent down with a special word from the manager commending him as a tried hand, equal to any post or service. The ditch superintendent was looking for such a man. He gave him those five crucial miles between the head-gates and Glenn's Ferry, the notorious beat that had sifted Finlayson's force without yet finding a man who could keep the banks. Some said it was the Arc-light saloon at Glenn's Ferry; some said it was the pretty girl at Lark's.

Whatever it was, Travis raged at it in the silent hours of his one-man watch; and the report had gone up the line now, three times since he had taken hold, of breaks on his division. And the engineer would by no means "weaken" on a question of the work, nor did the loyal watchman ask that any one should weaken, to spare him. He was all eyes and ears; he watched by daylight, he listened by dark, and the sounds that he heard in his dreams were sounds of water searching the banks, swirling and sinking into holes, or of mud subsiding with a wretched flop into the insidious current.

It was a queer country along the new ditch below the head-gates; as old and sun-bleached and bony as the stony valleys of Arabia Petrea; all but that strip of green that led the eye to where the river wandered, and that warm brown strip of sown land extending field by field below the ditch.

Lark's ranch was the first one below the head-gates, lying between the river and the ditch, an old homesteader's claim, sub-irrigated by means of rude dams ponding the natural sloughs. The worn-out land, never drained, was foul and sour, lapsing into swamps, the black alkali oozing and spreading from pools in its boggy pastures.

A few pioneer fruit-trees still bloomed and bore, undiscouraged by neglect, and cast homelike shadows on the weedy grass around the cabin and sheds that slouched at all angles, with nails starting and shingles warping in the sun.

Similar weather-stains and odd kicks and bulges the old rancher's person exhibited, when he came out to sun himself of a rimy morning, when cobwebs glittered on the short, late grass, and his joints reminded him that the rains were coming. And up and down the cow-trail below the ditch, morning and evening, went his dairy-herd to pasture; and after them loitered Nancy, on a strawberry pony with milk white mane and tail.

The lights and shadows chased her in and out among the willows and fleecy cottonwoods and tall swamp-grasses; but Travis rode in the glare, on the high ditch-bank, and, although they passed each other daily, he had never had a good look at the "pretty girl at Lark's." But one morning the white-faced heifer broke away and bolted up the ditch-bank, and in a cloud of sun-smitten dust Nancy followed, a figure of virginal wrath with scarlet cheeks and wind-blown hair. Reining her pony on the narrow bank, she called across to Travis in a voice as clear and fresh as her colors:—

"Head her off, can't you? *What* are you about!" This last to the pony, who was behaving "mean."

"Ride to the bridge and head her this way. I can drive her up the bank," Travis responded.

Nancy obeyed him, and waited at the bridge while he endeavored to persuade the heifer of the error of her ways. The heifer was not easily per-suaded, and Travis was wet to the waist before he had got her out; but he lost nothing of the bright figure guarding the bridge, a slender shape all pink and blue and dark blue, with hair like the sun on brown water, and a perfect seat, and a ringing voice calling thanks and bewildering encourage-ment to her ally in the stream. And this was old Solomon's daughter!

But "Oh, my Nancy!" the boys would groan, with excess of apprecia-tion beyond words, and for that Nancy heeded them not: and now Travis knew that the boys were right.

"Thank you ever so much!" her clear voice lilted, as the discomfited runaway dashed down the bank to the path she had forsaken. "I'm ever so sorry she dug all those bad tracks in the ditch. Will they do any harm?"

Travis assured her that nothing did harm if only it were known in time.

"What is the matter with it, anyhow—the ditch? Isn't it built right?"

"The ditch is the prettiest I ever saw," Travis responded, with all the warmth of his unrequited devotion to that faithless piece of engineering.

"All new ditches need watching till the banks get settled."

"Well, I should say that *you* watched! Don't you ever stir off that bank?"

"I eat and sleep sometimes."

"You must have a pretty dry camp up above. Wouldn't you like some milk once in a while?"

"Thanks; I never happened to fall in with the milkman on my beat."

"We have lots to spare, and buttermilk too, if you're not too proud to come for it. The others used to."

"I guess I don't quite catch on."

"The other watchmen, the boys who were here before you."

"Oh," said Travis coldly.

"Well, any time you choose to come down I'll save some for you," said the girl, as if that matter were settled.

"I'm afraid it is rather off my beat," Travis hesitated, "but I'm just as much obliged."

Nancy straightened herself haughtily. "Oh, it is nothing to be obliged for, if you don't care to come."

"I did not say I didn't care," Travis protested; but she was gone. The dust flew, and presently her dark blue skirt and the pony's silver tail flashed past the willows in the low grounds.

"I shall never see her again," he mourned. "So much for those other fellows spoiling her idea of a watchman's duty. Of course she thought I could come if I wanted to. Did she ask them, I wonder?"

Nancy was piqued, but not resentful. The more he did not come, as evening after evening smiled upon the level land; the more she thought of Travis, alone in his dusty camp, alone on his blinding beat; the more she dwelt upon the singularity and constancy of his refusal, the more she respected him for it.

So one day he did see her again. She was sitting on the bridge planks, leaning forward, her arms in her lap, her hat tipped back, a star of white sunlight touching her forehead. She lifted her head when she heard him coming and put her hand over her eyes, as if she were dizzy with watching the water.

"How's the ditch?" she called in a voice of sweetest cheer. She was on her feet now, and he saw how entrancing she was, in a blue muslin frock and a broad white hat with a wreath of pink roses bestrewing the tilted brim. Had they got company at the ranch? was his jealous reflection.

"How's the ditch behaving itself these days?" she repeated.

"Much as usual, thank you," Travis beamed from his saddle.

"Breaking, as usual?"

"Yes; it broke night before last."

"Well, I don't believe it's much of a ditch, anyhow. I wouldn't fret about it if I was you. Don't you think I'm very good-natured, after your snubbing me so? Here I've brought you a basket of apples, seeing you wouldn't spare time from your old ditch to come for them yourself. That in the napkin is a little pat of fresh butter." She lifted the grape-leaves that covered the basket. "I thought it might taste good in camp."

"Good! Well, I rather guess it will taste good! See here, I can't ever thank you for this—for bringing it yourself." He had few words, but his looks were moderately expressive.

Nancy blushed with pleasure. "Well, I had to—when folks are so wrapped up in their business. There, with Susan's compliments! Susan's the heifer you rounded up for me in the ditch. I know she made you a lot of work, tracking holes in your banks you're so fussy about. Do you really think it is a good ditch?"

"I am positive it is."

"Then if anything goes wrong down here they will lay the blame on you?"

"They are welcome to. That's what I am here for."

Nancy openly acknowledged her approval of a man that stood right up to his work and would take no odds of any one.

"The other boys were always complaining and saying it was the ditch. But there, I know it is mean of me to talk about them."

"I guess it won't go any further," said Travis dryly.

"Well, I hope not. They were good boys enough, but pretty trifling watchmen, I shouldn't wonder."

Travis had nothing to say to this, but he made a mental note or two.

"When will you give me a chance to return your basket?"

"Why, anytime; there's no hurry about the basket. Have you any regular times?"

He looked away, dissembling his joy in the question, and answered as if he were making an official report—

"I leave camp at six, patrol the line to the ferry and back, lay off an hour, and down again at eleven. Back in camp at three, and two hours for dinner. On again at five, and back in camp at nine. I pass this bridge, for instance, at seven and nine of a morning, twelve and two afternoons, and six and eight in the evening."

"Six and eight," Nancy mused, with a slight increase of color. "Well, I can stop some evening after cow-time, I suppose; but it isn't any matter about the basket."

Six evenings, going and coming, Travis delayed in passing the bridge, on the watch for Nancy; six times he filled the basket with such late field-flowers as he could find, and she never came. On the seventh evening his heart announced her, from as far off as his eyes beheld her. This time she was in white, without her hat, and she wore a blue ribbon in her gold-brown braids—a blue ribbon in her braids, and a red, red rose in either cheek; and her colors, and the colors of the sky, floated like flowers on the placid water.

"Well, where is the basket, then?" she merrily demanded.

"I left it behind, for luck."

"For luck? What sort of luck?"

"Six times I brought it, and you were never here; so tonight I just kicked it into the tent and came off without it. It seems to have been about the right thing to do."

"What, my basket!"

"Your basket. And it was filled with wild flowers, the prettiest I could find. It's your own fault for not coming before."

"I never set any day that I know of. I have been up to town."

Travis was not pleased to hear it.

"Yes; and I saw your company's manager. What a young man he is! I had no idea managers were ever young. And stylish—my! I'm sure I hope he'll know me when he sees me again," she added, coloring and dropping her eyes.

Travis grimly expressed the opinion that he probably would. Nancy continued to strike the wrong note with cruel precision; she could not have done better had she calculated her words; and all the while looking as innocent as the shining water under her feet—and that last time she had been so kind!

And the ditch was as provoking as Nancy, rewarding his devotion with breaks that defied all explanation. It was not possible that the patience of the management could hold out much longer; and when he should have been dismissed in disgrace from his post, Nancy would lightly class him as another of those "good boys enough, but trifling watchmen."

II

The first dry moon was just past the full. At nine o'clock the sky began to whiten above the long, bare ridge of the side-hill cut. At half past, the edge of the moon's disk clove the sky-line, and the shadow of the ridge crept down among the willows and tule-beds of the bottom. At ten the shadow had shrunk; it lay black on the ditch-bank, but the whispering tree-tops below were turning in silver light that flickered along the cow-path and caught the still eye of a dark, shallow pool among the tules.

Nancy had chosen this night for a stroll to the bridge, where Travis might be expected to pass, any time between eight o'clock and moonrise. Instead of Travis came a man whom she recognized as one of the watchmen from a lower division. He saluted her, after the custom of the country, claiming nothing on personal grounds but the privilege to look rather hard at the girlish figure silhouetted against the water. It was yet early enough for sky-gleams to linger on still pools, or to color the wimpling reaches of the ditch.

Nancy was disappointed; she had not come out to see a strange rider passing on Travis's gray horse. Her little plans were disconcerted. She had waited for what she considered a dignified interval, before seeming to take cognizance of her watchman's hours; now it appeared that the part of dignity might be overdone. Had Travis been superseded on his beat? She was conscious of missing him already. Her walk home, through the confidential willows, struck a chill of loneliness which the aspect of the house did not dispel. All was as dark and empty as she had left it. Was her father still at work at those tedious dams? This had been his given reason for frequent absences of late, after his usual working hours; though why he should choose the dark nights for mending his dams Nancy had not asked herself. Tonight she wanted him, or somebody, to drive away this queer new ache that made the moonlight too large and still for one little girl to wander in alone.

She searched for him. He was in none of the expected places; the dank fields were as empty as the house. She turned back to the ditch; from its high bank she could see farther into the shadowy places of the bottom.

Travis, meanwhile, had been leisurely pursuing his evening beat. He had overtaken one of his fellow-watchmen, on foot, walking to town, had lent him his horse for the last two miles to camp, and invited him to help himself to what he could find for supper, without waiting for his host.

"It is a still night," said Travis; "I'll mog along slowly up the ditch, and put in a little extra listening: it's at night the water talks."

Long after the rider had passed on, the tread of his horse's hoofs was heard, diminishing on the hard-tramped bank; a loosened stone rattled down and splashed into the water; the wind rustled in the tule-beds; then all surface sounds ceased, and the only talker was the ditch, chuckling and dawdling like an idle child on its errand, which it could not be persuaded to take seriously, to the desert lands.

Travis came to the ticklish spot near the bridge, and stopped to listen. Here the ditch cut through beds of clean sand, where the water might sink and work back into the old ground, the sand holding it like a sponge, till all the bottom became a bog, and the banks sank in one wide-spread, general wash-out. The first symptom of such deep-seated trouble would be the water's motion in the ditch—whirling round and round as if boring a hole in the bottom.

Travis laid his ear to the current, for he could judge of the water's movement by the sound. All seemed right at the bridge, but far up the ditch he was aware of a new demonstration. He listened awhile, and then walked on with long, light steps and gained upon the sound, which persisted, defining itself as a muffled churning at marked intervals, with now and then a wait between. The prodding was of some tool at work under water, at the ditch-bank.

He crossed to the upper side, and moved forward cautiously along the ridge, crouching that his figure might not be seen against the sky.

Nancy had gone up the cow-trail, past the low grounds, and was just climbing the bank when a dark shape, of man or beast, crashed down the opposite slope and shot like a slide of rock into the water.

A half-choked cry followed the plunge, then ugly sounds of a scuffle under the ditch-bank—men breathing hard, sighing and snorting; and somebody gasped as if he were being held down till his breath was gone.

"Get in there, you old muskrat! You shall stop your own breaks if it takes your cursed carcass to do it! Now then, have you got your breath?"

Nancy stayed only to hear a voice that was her father's, convulsed withterror and the chill of his repeated duckings, begging to be spared the anguish of drowning by night in three feet of ditch-water.

"Mr. Travis," she screamed, "you let my father be, whatever you are doing to him! Father, you come right home and get on dry clothes!"

Travis was as much amazed as if Diana with the moon on her forehead had appeared on the ditch-bank to take old Solomon Lark under her maiden protection; but no less he stuck to his prize of war.

"Your father hasn't time to change his clothes just yet, Miss Nancy; he's got some work to do first."

"Who are you, to be setting my father to work? Let go of him this minute! You are drowning him; you are choking him to death!" sobbed the frantic girl. The shadow fortunately withheld the details of her father's condition, but she had seen enough. Had Travis been drinking? Was the man bereft of his senses?

He was quite himself apparently—hideously cool, yet roused, and his voice cut like steel.

"You had better go home, Miss Nancy, and light a fire and warm a blanket for your father's bed. He'll be pretty cold before he gets through with this night's work."

After this cruel speech he took no more notice of Nancy, but leaped upon the ditch-bank and began hurling earth in great shovelfuls, patting the old man on the head with his cold tool whenever he tried to clamber up after him.

"You'd better not try *that*," he roared in a terrible voice that wounded Nancy like a blow. "Get in there, now! Puddle, puddle, or I'll have you buried to the ears in five minutes!"

It was shocking, hideous, like a horrible dream. The earth rattled down all about Solomon, and frequently upon him; the water was thick with mud, and the wretched old man tramped and puddled for dear life, helping to mend the hole which he had secretly dug where no eye could discover, till the water had fingered it and enlarged the mischief to a break.

It was the work of vermin, and as such Travis had treated his prisoner. Nancy felt the insult as keenly as she abhorred the cruelty. She fled, hysterical with wrath and despair at her own helplessness. But while she made ready the means of consolation at home, her thinking powers came back, and, between what she suspected and what she remembered, she was not wholly in the dark as to the truth between her father and Travis.

There was no one to warm Travis's blankets, when he fell back upon camp about daybreak, reeking with cold perspiration, soaked with ditch-water and sore in every muscle from his frenzy of shoveling. He had had no supper the night before; his guest had eaten all the cooked food, burned all his light-wood kindlings, and forgotten to cover the bread-pail, and his bread was full of sand. He didn't think much of those tenderfeet, who called themselves ditch-men, on that lower division where there was no work at all to speak of.

He began—worse comfort—to consider his police work from a daughter's point of view. Alas for himself and Nancy! His idyl of the ditch was shattered like the tender sky-reflections that bloomed on its still waters, and vanished when the waters were troubled. His own thoughts were as that roily pool where he had ducked the old man in the darkness. He overslept himself, after thinking he should not sleep at all, and started down his beat not until noon of the next day. Halfway to the bridge on the ditch-bank he met Nancy Lark. She gave him a note, which he dismounted to take, she vouchsafing no greeting, not even a look, and standing apart while he read it, with the air of a martyr to duty.

Mr. Travis—
    I am a death-struck man in consequence of your outrageous treatment of me last evening. I've took a dum chill, and it has hit me in the vitals through standing in water up to my armpits. If you think your fool ditch is worth more than a Human's life, though your company's enemy, that's for you to settle as you can when the time comes you'll have to. I don't ask any favors. But if you got anny desency left in you through working for that fish-livered company of bondholders coming out here to stomp us farmers into the dirt, you will call this bizness quits. I aint in no shape to fight ditches no more. You have put me where I be, and the less said on both sides the better, it looks to me. If that's so you can say so by word or writing. I should prefer writing as I aint got that confidence I might have.
    Yours truly,
    SOLOMON LARK

"Miss Nancy," said Travis gently, "is your father very sick this morning?"

"I don't know," Nancy replied.

"Have you sent for a doctor?"

"He won't let me."

"Have you read this letter?" She flashed an indignant look at him.

"I wish you would, then."

"It is not my letter. I don't know what's in it, and I don't care to know."

"Do you know what your father was doing in the ditch last night?"

"Helping you to mend it, at the risk of his life, because you made him," Nancy answered quickly.

"Helping to mend a hole he made himself, so there would be a nice little break in the morning."

The subject rested there, till Travis, forced to take the defensive, asked:—

"Do you believe me?"

"Believe what?"

"What I have just told you about your father?"

"Oh," she said, "it makes no difference to me. I knew my father pretty well before I ever saw you. If you think he was doing that, why, I suppose you will have to think so. But even if he was, I don't call that any reason you should half drown him, and make him work himself to death beside."

"But the water was warm! And I did the work. What was it to tread dirt for an hour or so on a summer's night? Wasn't he in the ditch when I found him?"

"I don't know, I'm sure," said Nancy. "I know that you kept him there."

"Well, I hope he'll keep out of the ditch after this. Working at ditches at night isn't good for his health. But you needn't be alarmed about him this time; I think he'll recover. But remember this: last night I was the company's watchman; I had an ugly piece of work to do and I did it; but, fair play or foul, whatever may happen between your father and me, remember, it is only my work, and you are not in it."

"Well, I guess I'm in it if my father is," said Nancy, "and that is something for you to remember."

"Oh, hang the work and the ditch and all the ditches!" thought Travis; yet it was the ditch that had put color and soul and meaning into his life—that had given him sight of Nancy. And it was not his work nor his convictions about it that stood between them now; it was her woman's contempt for justice and reason where her feelings were concerned. The case was simple as Nancy saw it; too simple, for it left him out in the cold. He would have had it complicated by a little more feeling in his direction.

"Well, have I got your answer?" she asked. "Father said I was to bring an answer, but not to let you come."

"He need not be afraid," said Travis bitterly. "If he will leave my ditch-banks alone, I shall not meddle with him. Tell him, if there are no more breaks there will be nothing to report. This break is mended—the break in the ditch, I mean."

"Then you will not tell?" Nancy stole a look at him that was half a plea.

"You would even promise to like me a little, wouldn't you, if you couldn't get the old man off any other way?" he mocked her sorrowfully.

"Well, I had rather have you hate me than stoop to coax me, as I've seen girls do—"

He might be satisfied, she passionately answered; she hated him enough. She hated his work, and the hateful way he did it.

"You are an unmerciful man!" she accused him, with a sob in her voice. "You don't know the trouble my father has had; how many years he has worked, with nothing but his hands; and now your company comes and claims the water, and turns the river, that belongs to everybody, into their big ditch. I'd like to know how they came to own this river! And when they have got it all in their ditch, all the little ditches and the ponds will go dry. We were here years before any of you ever thought of coming, or knew there was a country here at all. It's claim-jumping; and not a cent will they pay, and laugh at us besides, and call us mossbacks. I don't blame my father one bit, if he did break the ditch. If you are here to watch, then watch!—watch me! Perhaps you think I've had a hand in your breaks?"

Travis turned pale. He had made the mistake of trying to reason with Nancy, and now he felt that he must go on, in justice to his case, though she was far away from all his arguments, rapt in the grief, the wrath, the conviction, of her plea.

"You talk as women talk who only hear one side," he replied. "But you people down here don't know the company's intentions; they don't ask, and when they do they won't believe what they are told. That talk against companies is an old politicians' drive. This country is too big for single men to handle; companies save years of waiting. This one will bring the railroads and the markets, and boom up the price of land. The ditch your father hates so will make him a rich man in five years, if he does nothing but sit still and let it come.

"As for water, why do you cry before you are hurt? Nobody can steal a river. That is more politicians' talk, to make out they are the settlers' friends. We are the settlers' friends, because we are the friends of the country's boom; it can't boom without us. Why should *I* believe in this company? I'm a poor man, a settler like your father. I've got land of my own, but I can see we farmers can't do everything for ourselves; it's cheaper to pay a company to help us. They are just peddlers of water, and we buy it. Who owns the other, then? Don't we own them just as much as they own us?

"Come, if you can't feel it's so, leave hating us at least till we have done all these things you accuse us of. Wait till we take all the water and ruin your land. Most of these farmers along the river have got too much water; they are ruining their own land. So I tell your father, but he thinks he knows it all."

"He is some older than you are, anyhow."

"He is too old to be working nights in ditches. Tell him so from me, will you?"

"Oh, I'll tell him! I don't think you will be troubled much with us around your ditch, after this. I went to the bridge last night because I thought you were nice, and a friend. I had a respect for you more than for any of the others. I might have come to think better of the ditch; but I've had all the ditch I want, and all the watchmen. Never, till I die, shall I forget how my father looked," she passionately returned to the charge. "An old man like him! Why didn't you put me in and make me tread dirt for you? The water was *warm*; and I'm enough better able than he was!"

"I'll get right down here and let you tread on me, and be proud to have you, if it will cure the sight of what you saw me do last night. I was mad, don't you understand? I have to answer for all this foolishness of your father's, remember. It had to be stopped."

"Was there no way to stop it but half drowning him, and insulting him besides?"

"Yes, there is another way; inform the company, and have him shut up in the Pen. *I* thought I let the old man off pretty easy. But if you prefer the other way, why, next time there's a break, we can try it."

"I'm sure we ought to thank you for your kindness," said Nancy. "And if we are Companied out of house and home, and father made a criminal, we shall thank you still more. Good-morning."

Their eyes met and hers fell. She turned away, and he remounted and rode on up the ditch, angry, as a man can be only with one he might have loved, down to those dregs of bitterness that lurk at the bottom of the soundest heart.

III

He was but an idle watchman all that day, so sure he was that the ditch was right and Solomon the author of all his troubles; and Solomon was "fixed" at last. Weariness overcame him, and at the end of his beat he slept, under the lee of the ditch-bank, instead of returning to his camp.

Next morning he was riding along at his usual pace when it struck him how incredibly the ditch had fallen. The line of silt that marked the water's normal depth now stood exposed and dry, full two feet above its running, and the pulse of the current had weakened as though it were ebbing fast.

He put his horse to a run, and lightened ship as he went, casting off his sack of oats, then his coat and such tools as he could spare; he might have been traced to the scene of disaster by his impedimenta strewing the ditch-bank.

The water had had hours the start of him; its work was sickening to behold. A part of the bank had gone clean out, and the ditch was returning to the river by way of Solomon Lark's alfalfa fields. The homestead itself was in danger.

He cut sage-brush and tore up tules by the roots, and piled them as a wing-dam against the outer bank, and heaped dirt like mad upon the mats; and as he worked, alone, where forty men were needed, came Nancy, with glowing face, flying down the ditch-bank, calling the word of exquisite relief:—

"I've shut off the water. Was that right?"

Right! He had been wishing himself two men, nay, three: one at the bank, and one at the gates, and one carrying word to Finlayson.

"Can I do anything else?"

"Yes; make Finlayson's camp quick as you can," Travis panted over a shovelful of dirt he was heaving.

"Yes; what shall I tell him?"

"Tell him to send up everything he has got; every man and team and scraper."

Nancy was gone, but in a few moments she was back again, wringing her hands, and as white as a cherry-blossom.

"The water is all down round the house, and father is alone in bed crying like a child."

"There's nothing to cry about now. You turned off the water; see, it has almost stopped."

"Can I leave him with you?"

"Great Scott! I'll take care of him! But go, there's a blessed girl. You will save the ditch."

Nancy went, covering the desert miles as a bird flies; she exulted in this chance for reparation. But long after Finlayson's forces had arrived and gone to work, she came lagging wearily homeward, all of a color, herself and the pony, with the yellow road. She had refused a fresh horse at the ditch-camp, and, sparing the whip, reached home not until after dark.

Her father's excitement in his hours of loneliness had waxed to a pitch of childish frenzy. He wept, he cursed, he counted his losses, and when his daughter said, to comfort him, "Why, father, surely they must pay for this!" he threw himself about in his bed and gave way to lamentations in which the secret of his wildness came out. He had done the thing himself; and he dared not risk suspicion, and the investigation that would follow a heavy claim for damages.

Nancy could not believe him. "Father, do be quiet; you didn't do any such thing," she insisted. "How could you, when I know you haven't stirred out of this bed since night before last? Hush, now; you are dreaming; you are out of your head."

"I guess I know what I done. I ain't crazy, and I ain't a fool. I made this hole first, before he caught me at the upper one. I made this one to keep him busy on his way up, so's the upper one could get a good start. The upper one wouldn't 'a' hurt us. It's jest like my cussed luck! I knew it was a-comin', but I didn't think I'd get it like this. It's all his fault, the great lazy loafer, sleepin' at the bottom of his beat, 'stead o' comin' up as he'd ought to have done last evening. He wasted the whole night—and calls himself a watchman!"

"Well, I'm glad of it," Nancy cried excitedly. "I'm just *glad* we are washed out, and I hope this will end it!" and she burst into tears, and ran out of the room.

She sat by herself, weeping and storming, in the dark little shed-room.

"Nancy!" she heard her father calling, "Nancy, child! . . . Where's that gal taken herself off to? . . . Are you a-settin' up your back on account of that ditch? If you are, you ain't no child of mine. . . . I'm dum sorry I let on a word to her about it. How do I know but she's off with it now, to that watchman feller. I'll be put in the papers—an old man informed on by his darter, and he on his last sick bed! . . . Nancy, I say, where be you a-hidin' yourself?"

Nancy returned to her forlorn charge, and after a while the old man fell asleep. She put out the lamp, for she could see to move about the room by the light of the sage-brush bonfires that flared along the ditch, lighting the men and teams, all Finlayson's force, at work upon the broken banks.

The sight was wild and alluring; she went out to watch the strange army of shadows shifting and intermingling against a wall of flame.

There was a distressful space to cross, of sand and slippery mud and drowned vegetation, including the remains of her garden; the look of everything was changed. Only the ditch-bank against the reddened sky supplied the usual landmark. Its crest was black with shovelers, and up and down in lurid light climbed the scraper-teams; climbed and dumped, and dropped over the bank to climb again, like figures in a stage procession. There was a bedlam roar and crackle of pitchy fires, rattle of harness, clank of scraper-pans, shouts of men to the cattle, oaths and words of command; and this would go forward unceasingly till the banks held water. And what was the use of contending?

Nancy felt bitterly the insignificance of such small scattered folk as her father, pitiful even in their spite. Their vengeance was like the malice of field-mice or rabbits, which the farmers fenced out of their fields into the desert where they belonged. What could such as they do either to help or hinder this invincible march of capital into the country where they, with untold hardships, had located the first claims? And some of them were ready enough, for a little temporary relief, to part with their birthright to these clever sons of Jacob.

"Out we go, to find some other wilderness for them to take away from us! We are only mossbacks," said the daughter of Esau.

As she spoke, half aloud to herself, a man rushed past her down the bank, flattened himself on his hands, laid his face to the water, and drank and paused to pant, and drank again, while she could have counted a score. Then he lifted his head, sighed, and stretched himself back with a groan of complete exhaustion.

The firelight touched his face, and showed her Travis: haggard, hollow-eyed, soaked with ditch-water, and matted with mud, looking as if he had been dragged bodily through the ditch-bank, like thread through a piece of cloth.

Nancy did not try to avoid him.

"Oh, is it you?" he marveled, softly smiling up at her. "What a splendid ride you made! Did nobody thank you? Finlayson said he couldn't find you when he was leaving camp."

Nancy answered not a word; she was trembling so that she feared to betray herself by speaking.

"I was coming to say good-by, when I had washed my face," he continued. "I got my time tonight."

"Your time?"

"My time-check. They are going to put another man in my place. So you needn't hate me any longer on account of the ditch; you can transfer all that to the next fellow."

"Isn't that just like them? They never can do anything fair!"

"Like who? Do you suppose I'm going to kick about it? The only wonder is they kept me on so long."

Every word of Travis's was a knife in Nancy's conscience, to say nothing of her pride. She hugged her arms in her shawl, and rocked herself to and fro. Travis crawled up the bank a little way further, and stretched himself humbly beside her. The dark shadows under his aching eyes started a pang of pity in the girl's heart, sore beset as she was with troubles of her own.

"I'm glad it's duskish," he remarked, "so you can't see the sweet state I'm in. I'm all over top-soil. You might rent me to a Chinaman for twenty-five dollars an acre; and I don't need any irrigating either."

An irresponsible laugh from Nancy was followed by a sob. Then she gathered herself to speak.

"See here, do you want to stay on this ditch?"

"Of course I do. I wanted to stay till I had straightened out my own record, and shown what the ditch can do. But no management under heaven could stand such work as this."

"Then stay, if you want to. You have only to say the word. You said you'd inform if there was a next time, and there is. Father did it. He made this break, too; he made them both the same night, and didn't dare to tell of this one. Now, go and clear yourself and get back your beat."

"Are you sure of this you are telling me?"

"Well, I guess so. It isn't the sort of thing I'd be likely to make up. And I say you can tell if you want to. I make you a present of the information. If father isn't willing to take the consequences, I am; and they half belong to me. I won't have anybody sheltering us, or losing by us. We have got no quarrel with you."

"That is brave of you. I wish it was something more than brave," sighed Travis. "But I want it all myself. I can't spare this information to the company. You didn't do it for them, did you?"

"When I go telling on my father to save a ditch, I guess it will be after now," said Nancy. "If that rich company, with all its men and watchmen and teams and money, can't protect itself from one poor old man—"

"Never mind the company," said Travis. "What's mine is mine. This word you gave to me, it doesn't belong to my employers. You have saved me to myself; now I shall not go kicking myself for sleeping that night on my beat. It's not so bad—oh, not half so bad—for me!"

"Then go tell them, and get the credit for it. Don't you mean to?"

She could not see him smile. "When I tell, you will hear of it."

"But you talked about your record."

"I shall have to go to work and make a new record. Ah, if you would be as kind as you are brave! Was it all just for pride you told me this? Don't you care, not the least bit, about my part—that I am down and out of everything?"

"It's your own fault, then. I have told you how you can clear yourself and stay."

"And lose my chance with you! I was thinking of coming back, some day, to tell you—what you must know already. Nancy, you do know!"

"You forget," shivered Nancy; "I am the daughter of the man you called—"

"Is that fair—to bring that up now?"

"You mustn't deceive yourself. There are some things that can't be forgotten."

"How did *I* know what I was saying? A man isn't always responsible."

"I heard you," said Nancy. "There are things we say when we are raging mad at a person, and there are things we say when we think them the dirt under our feet. You kept him down with your dirt-shovel, and you called him—what I can't ever forget."

"And is this the only hitch between us?"

"I should think it was enough. Who despises my father despises me."

"But I do not despise him," Travis did not scruple to assert. "The quarrel was not mine; and I'm not a ditch-man any longer. I will apologize to your father."

"Oh, I know it costs you nothing to apologize. You don't mind father—an old man like him! You'd take him in, and give him his meals, and pat him on the head as you would the house-dog that bites because he's old and cross. Well, I'll let you know I don't want you to forgive him, and apologize, and all that stuff. I want you to get even with him."

"Be satisfied," said Travis. "The only count I have against your father is through his daughter. There is no way for me to get even with you. And when you have spoiled a man's life just for one angry word—"

"Not angry," she interrupted. "I could have forgiven you that."

"For one word, then. And you call it square when you have given me a piece of information to use for myself, against you! I will go back now and go to work. They can't say I haven't earned my wages on this beat."

He looked down at her, longing to gather her, with all her thorny sweetness, to his breast; but her attitude forbade him.

"Can't we shake hands?" he said. They shook hands in silence, and he went back and finished the night in the ranks of the shovelers—to work well, to love well, and to get his discharge at last. Yet Travis was not sorry that he had taken those five miles below Glenn's Ferry: he had found something to work for.

The company's officials marveled, as the weeks went by, that nothing was heard of Solomon Lark. He had ever been the sturdiest beggar for damages on the ditch. If he lacked an occasion he could invent one; he was known to be a fanatic on the subject of the small farmers' wrongs: yet now, with a veritable claim to sue for, the old protestant was dumb. Had Solomon turned the other cheek? There were jokes about it in the office; they looked to have some fun with Solomon yet.

In the early autumn the joking ceased. There was a final reason for the old man's silence—Solomon was dead. His ranch was rented to a Chinese vegetable-gardener who bought water from the ditch.

The company, through its officials, was disposed to recognize this unspoken claim that had perished on the lips of the dead. They made an estimate, and offered Nancy Lark a fair sum in consideration of her father's losses by the ditch.

It was unusual for a company to volunteer a settlement of this kind; it was still more unusual for the indemnity to be refused. Nancy declined, by letter, first; then the manager asked her to call at the office. She did not come. He took pains to hunt her up at the house of her friends in town. He might have delegated the call, but he chose to make it in person, and was struck by an added dignity, a finer beauty in the saddened face of the girl whom he remembered as a bit of a rustic coquette.

He went over the business with her. She was perfectly intelligent in the matter; there had been no misunderstanding. Why then would she not take what belonged to her? Companies were not in the habit of paying claims that were claims of sentiment.

"I have made no claim," said Nancy.

"But you have one. You inherited one. We do not propose to rob—"

She put out her hand with a gesture of appeal.

"My father had no claim. He never made one, nor meant to make one. I am the best judge of what belongs to me. I don't want this money, and I will never take one cent of it. But there is a claim you can settle, if you are hunting up claims. It won't cost you anything," she faltered, as if some unguarded impulse had hurried her into a subject that she hardly knew how to go on with. She moved her chair back a little from the light.

"There was one of your watchmen, on the Glenn's Ferry beat, who lost his place on account of those breaks coming one after another—"

"Yes," said the manager; "there were several that did. Which man do you refer to?"

The name, she thought, was Travis. Then, blushing, she spoke out courageously:—

"It was Mr. Travis. He was discharged just after the big break. You thought it was his carelessness, but it was not. I am the only one that can say so, and I know it. You lost the best watchman you ever had on the ditch when you took his name off your pay-roll. He worked for more than just his money's worth, and it hurt him to lose that place."

"Are you aware that he made the worst record of any man on the line?"

"I don't care what his record was; he kept a good watch. It's no concern of mine to say so," she said. Trembling and red and white, the tears shining in her honest eyes, she persisted: "He had his reasons for never explaining, and they were nothing to be ashamed of. I think you might believe me!"

"I do," said the manager, willing to spare her. "I will attend to the case of Mr. Travis when I see him. I do not think he has left the country. In fact, he was inquiring about you only the other day, in the office, and he seemed very much concerned to hear of your—of the loss you have suffered. Shall I say that you spoke a good word for him?"

"You need not do that," she answered with spirit. "He knows whether he kept watch. But you may say that I ask, as a favor, that he will answer all your questions; and you need not be afraid to question him."

Travis was given back his beat, but no more explicit exoneration would he accept. The reason of his reinstatement was not made public, and naturally there was gossip about it among other discharged watchmen who had not been invited to try again.

Two of these cynic philosophers, popularly known as sore-heads, foregathered one morning at Glenn's Ferry and began to discuss the management and the ditch.

"Travis don't seem to have so much trouble with the water this year as he had last," the first ex-watchman remarked. "Used to get away with him on an average once a week, so I hear."

"He's married his girl," the other explained sarcastically. "He's got more time to look after the ditch."

There is no sand, now, in Travis's bread; the prettiest girl on the ditch makes it for him, and walks beside him when the lights are fair and the shadows long on the ditch-bank. And it is a pleasure to record that both

Nancy and the ditch are behaving as dutifully as girls and water can be expected to do, when taken from their self-found paths and committed to the sober bounds of responsibility.

Flowers bloom upon its banks, heaven is reflected in its waters, fair and broad are the fertile pastures that lie beyond; but the best-trained ditch can never be a river, nor the gentlest wife a girl again.

THE END